Cinnamon

The Black Cat Detectives

Wendy Meddour

F

FRANCES LINCOLN
CHILDREN'S BOOKS

The Missing Piece

It all began when Iqbal Stalk got a chess piece stuck up his nose. Until that sticky moment, nothing much was happening in Cinnamon Grove. Blackbirds were cluttering up the telephone wires, clouds were drifting over chimney pots and lazy-day dads were mowing weed-speckled lawns. The holidays had begun. No school. No homework. No worries. Just long, empty days stretching across the summer like a yawn.

"CHECKMATE," beamed a wiry little girl with glasses.

"That is *so* not fair," groaned Ramzi. He was fed up with losing – even if it *was* to Shaima Stalk.

Hmmmpph.

5

"What was that?" asked Ramzi, his head swivelling round.

"What?" Shaima leant forward to listen.

HMMMPHHH.

There it was again! Only this time, the noise was louder.

"It's coming from behind the sofa," whispered Ramzi. He stood up and tiptoed across the carpet. Shaima followed. They crept on to the cushions and peered over the top.

A tiny little boy stared up at them, clutching his nose very tight.

"*Iqbal,*" groaned Shaima, catching her slipping spectacles. "What have you done *now*?"

"Nothing. It just f...f...fell up," stammered Iqbal.

"*What* fell up?" asked Ramzi.

"*Nothing* did," Iqbal cried.

"MUM," yelled Shaima, " Iqbal's got a chess piece stuck up his nose!"

"How do you know that?" asked Ramzi, peering over the sofa. Iqbal was still clutching his face tight.

"Just a simple process of deduction," said Shaima. "I noticed a missing chess piece earlier and Iqbal's *always* putting things up his nose."

"Is he?" asked Ramzi, looking down at Iqbal. His eyes were filling with water.

"Yeh. It's quite normal. It's a recognised toddler phase."

Ramzi didn't look convinced.

Just then, Mrs Stalk appeared in the doorway. Her peach-coloured sari sparkled in the sunlight as she scooped Iqbal into her arms.

"Iqbal Stalk," she said kindly. "How many times must I tell you,

noses are for sniffing, not stuffing. What have you done this time?"

"It was only an accident, *Ammi,*" whimpered Iqbal.

Mrs Stalk prised Iqbal's hand off his nose. "*Subhan'Allah!*" she exclaimed.

"Let me see, let me see," said Shaima eagerly. Jumping off the sofa, she rubbed her glasses and peered into the puffy darkness. "I knew it!" she said. "It's a pawn!"

"Then we'll need a bag of frozen chickpeas," said Mrs Stalk, carrying Iqbal into the kitchen.

"Chickpeas?" asked Ramzi, puzzled.

"To keep the swelling down," explained Shaima.

Mrs Stalk perched Iqbal on a stool and dug about in the freezer.

Shaima looked at Ramzi and grinned. Her eyes were sparkling. They always did that when she had a plan. "Back in a minute!" she cried, diving into the cupboard under the stairs. There was a CRASH and a BANG and a RUSTLE. Moments later, Shaima staggered out of the cupboard carrying an enormous black box.

"If I ... sterilise ... the ... pliers," she puffed, her

tiny body struggling under the weight, "I can make ... the ... extraction ... myself."

"No. You cannot," said Mrs Stalk firmly. "Now put your father's tool kit away."

"*Ammi,*" moaned Shaima. But she pushed the tool kit back into the cupboard.

"Hold these against Iqbal's nose," said Mrs Stalk, passing Ramzi the chickpeas. He pressed them gently against Iqbal's nose while Mrs Stalk searched in the folds of her sari. "I know it's in here somewhere," she said. "Ah, got it." She pulled out her mobile phone and texted Aunty Urooj. "She'll know what to do."

SALEM —
NEED U NOW
IQBAL IN TROUBLE!
PLS BRING TWEEZERS

"Is she a doctor or something?" asked Ramzi, the melting ice dripping down his arm.

"Kind of," grinned Shaima. "Just wait. You'll see."

Beetles and Tweezers

"*Salaams,* everyone," beamed Aunty Urooj, striding into the house. She wore a long velvet jacket, a beetle-print headscarf and a pair of high-heeled burgundy boots.

"*Alhamdulillah!*" said Mrs Stalk. "Have you brought your equipment?"

"Of course," smiled Aunty Urooj, patting the enormous carpet bag hanging from her shoulder. "I'll just slip off my boots."

While Aunty Urooj was undoing her laces, Shaima threw herself round her waist. "And it's good to see you too," laughed Aunty Urooj, squeezing Shaima hard. "But who's your friend?"

Ramzi was hovering in the hall, grinning awkwardly.

"You know … he's the one I told you about," began Shaima, "… with the sleepwalking Dad and the cute baby sister."

"So, *you're* the famous Ramzi Ramadan, are you?" winked Aunty Urooj.

Ramzi nodded and blushed.

"Come on then. Show me to the patient," she said, rubbing her hands together.

"He's in the kitchen," said Ramzi, leading the way.

***

"What *have* you done?" gasped Aunty Urooj. Iqbal's face was inflating like a little balloon. She tipped back his head and looked up his nose.

"I don't even know!" cried Iqbal.

"Judging by the small circle of green felt," said Shaima, "we're pretty sure it's a pawn."

"Excellent," said Aunty Urooj. She rolled up her sleeves. "Right, no time to lose. Amira, get me some olive oil."

Mrs Stalk poured some thick golden oil into a mug.

"Shaima – a torch."

Shaima ran upstairs.

"Iqbal – suck this." Aunty Urooj popped a bright red lollipop into Iqbal's mouth. "Now, where are my tweezers?" she said, rummaging in her carpet bag.

That's when Ramzi saw it! He completely and utterly froze. There was something scurrying up Aunty Urooj's arm. Something large and spindly and black! Ramzi gulped and took a step backwards. The *thing* had six twig-like legs and two gigantic antennae. Pointing at Aunty Urooj's arm, Ramzi let out a stifled scream.

"I've got them," said Aunty Urooj, waving some tiny little tweezers in the air.

Ramzi blinked. Couldn't she see it? Or was he dreaming? But how could he be? He wasn't even asleep. No. There was definitely a HUGE insect on Aunty Urooj's arm.

"Back inside, little one," cooed Aunty Urooj.

The creature stopped, turned round and crawled back down her sleeve. Ramzi blinked again. It had gone.

"What *was* that ...?" he asked.

Aunty Urooj was about to answer when Shaima burst into the kitchen.

"I've got the torch," she panted. Ramzi noticed a black notebook tucked under her arm. He'd seen it before – on the night Dad got stuck up a tree.

"Then we're ready," smiled Aunty Urooj. She pushed her bangles up her sleeves. "Now – watch and learn."

Shaima threw her notepad on to the work surface and scribbled:

Removal of obstruction
from Iqbal Stalk's Nose

"Shaima, stop writing me down!" cried Iqbal.

But Shaima wrote *everything* down. For her, life was one big experiment. It had to be observed, analysed and recorded. Shoving the pen behind her ear, she pointed the torchlight up Iqbal's nose. Aunty Urooj dipped the tweezers in olive oil. Then she told Iqbal to suck hard and look at the ceiling.

Pop!

It was all over in seconds.

"Ta taaaa," smiled Aunty Urooj, dropping the dripping little pawn on to the table.

"Iqbal's nose all better," grinned Iqbal.

"*Alhamdulillah,*" sighed Mrs Stalk. "And well done, Urooj!"

Aunty Urooj wiped her tweezers with some kitchen roll and took a little bow. Shaima and Ramzi clapped.

"Now, promise not to do it again," said Mrs Stalk.

"Can I promise *tomorrow*?" yawned Iqbal. "All of me's sleepy now."

Everyone laughed as Mrs Stalk hoisted him on to her hip. "Yes," she said, "it's time for your midday nap. In fact, after this morning, I think we could *all* do with a little rest!"

Truly Deeply Muslims

Moments later, Iqbal was asleep upstairs, Mrs Stalk was chopping onions and Aunty Urooj and Shaima were talking by the sink. But Ramzi didn't mind. In fact, he liked listening to the bubble of a language he didn't understand.

Strange words, fast and light, soon filled up the kitchen and Ramzi closed his eyes. He breathed in the spicy smells that wafted out of Mrs Stalk's pan. Then he took a deep breath and imagined himself in a far-off land ... Pakistan ... India ... Bangladesh ... He drew their wiggly outlines in his mind.

Opening one eye, he looked around. No. He was *still* in Cinnamon Grove and they were *still* chatting, so he jumped off his stool and wandered over to the shelves. They were laden with pots, all tightly packed with Mrs Stalk's potions and herbs. Craning his neck, Ramzi read the labels.

He glanced back at Mrs Stalk, who was stirring her enormous pan. She reminded him of a magician – with her billowing sari and her big wooden spoon. Only she didn't make spells. She made deep orange curries that made your eyes water and your throat tingle. Dad said Mrs Stalk's curries were the best in the world.

"*Come on,*" said Shaima, pulling Ramzi's arm. "Stop *dreaming*. I want to show you something."

Ramzi let her drag him into Mr Stalk's study where she flicked open the laptop. She clicked on 'favourites' and images of distant galaxies filled the screen.

"That is *so* cool!" said Ramzi, gazing at the

swirling, multicoloured light. He'd go there one day. Into space and beyond.

From the corner of the study, Aunty Urooj let out a big sigh. Ahhhhhh. She was flicking through some Persian poetry by the bookcase. Shaima and Ramzi looked up. She sighed again. AHHHHHHH.

"Are you OK?" asked Shaima.

Aunty Urooj nodded and adjusted her beetle-print headscarf. *Beetles*. How could Ramzi have forgotten? He *had* to ask:

"Errmm... Urooj... what was that *thing* in the kitchen? The one that crawled out of your bag?"

"Thing?" exclaimed Aunty Urooj, closing the book with a *SNAP*. "It wasn't a *thing*. It was an extremely rare Long-Horned Capricorn Beetle."

"Awesome!" exclaimed Shaima, leaping up from Mr Stalk's leather chair. "Did you bring it with you?"

"It's not an 'it'. It's a 'he'," she said, disappearing into the hall.

"She's probably gone to check on him," said Shaima.

"But why does she keep a beetle in her bag?" asked Ramzi.

"It's her job. Beetles and stuff. You know."

But Ramzi didn't know. He shrugged his shoulders.

"She's an insectologist," explained Shaima. "She studies insects."

"You mean, like, *bugs*. That's her *job*? No way!"

"*Ahem*," coughed Aunty Urooj. She was standing right behind them, stroking her enormous carpet bag. "His name is Gulliver," she said.

"You've called the beetle *Gulliver*? That is so weird," laughed Ramzi. "Beetles aren't supposed to have names."

"Yes, they are," said Shaima.

Aunty Urooj smiled kindly. "It's all right, Shaima. I'm probably the first insectologist Ramzi's ever met." She looked at Ramzi. "The thing is, Gulliver's one of the very few Long-Horned Capricorn Beetles left in Britain."

"What? Are there more?" asked Ramzi, edging away from the bag.

"Yes, isn't it wonderful?" said Aunty Urooj. "They were thought to be extinct until last year. But then, in a dusty corner of a furniture shop in Llanelli, one crept out of its hiding place."

"What happened?" asked Shaima.

Aunty Urooj bit her lip. "There were screams. People didn't know what to do. And tragically, the dear creature met a premature end. But it wasn't all sadness. What this unfortunate incident proved..." she leant forward, "was that the British Long-Horned Capricorn Beetle had *not* died out!" She grinned victoriously.

"So there are more?" said Ramzi nervously.

"Oh, yes. Lurking in old furniture. Hiding under stairs. Crawling around in cupboards. There *might* even be one under your bed. "

The blood drained from Ramzi's cheeks. He didn't mind *ordinary*-sized bugs. In fact, he quite liked them. But HUGE ones! That was different.

"U...under m...my b...bed?" he stammered.

"If you're lucky," said Aunty Urooj. "But remember, it took me over a year to find one." She turned to Shaima. "It's all thanks to your Aunty Zakiya, really. It was in one of her old commodes. And here he is! Sleeping soundly." She stroked the bag again.

"Can I see him?" asked Shaima, staring at the bag.

"I'd like to, Shaima, really I would. But he needs to get his rest."

"But he's just a beetle," said Ramzi.

"*Just a beetle*!" Aunty Urooj guffawed. She leant over to whisper in Ramzi's ear. "In Gulliver's natural habitat," she said, "his life expectancy would be short. But if I give him plenty of rest, then perhaps... just perhaps..." Her voice trailed off.

Ramzi smirked. He wasn't sure if she was being serious or not.

"There – see!" Shaima was pointing at the screen:

Academic Staff

Dr Urooj Stalk is one of Britain's leading insectologists. Currently researching Endangered Beetles of Britain, she has spent the last three years lecturing at Rocksford University. Of international renown, her work has been published in journals such as *Dung Beetles Digest*, *Weevils Weekly* and *Buzz: an International Journal of Insectology*.

COMPIX 2012

"Shaima!" hissed Aunty Urooj. "That's confidential. At least, until I've presented my paper in Dusseldorf..."

"Sorry. But your life's totally awesome. Just imagine..." Shaima eyes misted over, "presenting papers to lecture theatres full of brilliant scientists..."

"... and having a bag full of bugs!" laughed Ramzi.

Shaima snapped the laptop shut. "Exactly," she said.

Aunty Urooj sighed again. "It's not as 'awesome' as you might think," she said quietly.

"What do you mean?" asked Shaima.

"Nothing. It doesn't matter. You wouldn't understand."

"But Shaima understands *everything*," grinned Ramzi. "That's why they call her 'the walking encyclopaedia' at school. *Ouch*!" Shaima had just elbowed him in the ribs.

"*What* won't I understand, Aunty Urooj?" she asked.

"Oh, it's just grown-up stuff. Forget it."

But Shaima and Ramzi stared at her expectantly.

"OK. I'll tell you. It's just that... well...

I'm lonely. There. I've said it."

"How can you be lonely when you've got your beetles?" exclaimed Shaima.

"I know," nodded Aunty Urooj. "I love my beetles. But... it's just that...well... to put it bluntly... sometimes beetles aren't enough!"

Shaima gasped. "But you have 187 different varieties – including a Pakistani Tiger Beetle that can run at 8km per hour. Technically, if you take its size into account, that makes it the fastest land-running animal on the planet!"

"Shaima – don't be dim," said Ramzi.

"What?"

"She's right. I'm being silly. Come on, Gulliver." Aunty Urooj stroked her carpet bag and hurried into the kitchen.

"I don't get it," whispered Shaima.

"At last – something Shaima Stalk *doesn't* 'get'," grinned Ramzi. "She means..." He blushed. "She's *lonely*. Get it now?"

Shaima's eyes sparkled as the penny finally dropped. "Well, why didn't she say so?" Flipping open the laptop again she typed in MUSLIM MARRIAGE UK.

"What are you doing?" asked Ramzi, trying to hide the screen.

"Finding Aunty Urooj a husband, of course," said Shaima.

"You can't just *find* someone a husband!" whispered Ramzi.

"Why not?"

Ramzi grappled for an answer. "Because... because... because her parents have to do it."

"You mean *my grandparents*?" Shaima laughed. "Don't be silly. Nanna doesn't know anyone here apart from the chiropodist. And *Daada* ... well, he's gone – *rahemahullah*."

Ramzi chewed on his lip. "What about your dad?" he asked.

"He's way too busy at *The Spice Pot*. Oh, this looks good," said Shaima.

Truly Deeply Muslims
ONLINE MARRIAGE SERVICES

flashed up on the screen.

"Are you serious?" asked Ramzi.

"Yeh. 'Course. I *always* am!" grinned Shaima.

Don't Wake the Baby!

Back at Number Thirty-Two, Cinnamon Grove, Mrs Ramadan was in a mess. Baby wipes were strewn across the floor and there was a faint smell of sick in the air. "Did you have a good time at Shaima's?" she asked, pushing back her unbrushed hair.

Ramzi looked at the soggy wet patch on her shoulder.

"Baby Zed's not keeping her milk down," Mum sighed. "And I feel about one hundred and four."

"Don't worry, Mum," smiled Ramzi. "I'll make you a coffee. I know how."

"I know you do, love. All right. But make it a chamomile tea," said Mum. "According to the midwife, it helps to soothe the baby." She joggled the screaming bundle of pink blankets against her shoulder.

"BURRRRP."

"Better out than in," smiled Mum, patting Baby Zed's back. Then she wandered across the room and crumpled on to the sofa – the bundle of blankets held tight in her arms.

Very softly, Baby Zed started to snore. "*Sssssssss.*"

"Mum," whispered Ramzi, "I think she's gone to sleep."

Mum closed her eyes and smiled.

***

When Ramzi came back with the tea, Mum had fallen asleep too. He put the mug down and took Baby Zed out of her arms.

"Hello, little caterpillar," he said, stroking his baby sister's thistledown hair. He popped her in the wicker basket in the corner of the room and then put a blanket over Mum.

She looked different, somehow. Not like Awake-Mum. Asleep-Mum's face was flushed, her hand tucked under her cheek. Ramzi went and got his notebook from his rucksack. It had been Shaima's idea – to write things down. But his notebook wasn't like hers. His was messy – full of sketches, maps and thoughts – not neat little experiments and tidy observations. He scribbled down the word: SLEEP. Then he looked at Mum again.

Sleep is weird :
It makes Dad's dreams spill out.
But it makes Mum look different
Kind of like a child
What does it do to me?

Suddenly Ramzi looked worried. He tiptoed over to the wicker basket and peered inside. Baby Zed was *still* pink. She was *still* snoring. She *still* looked the same. Ramzi breathed a sigh of relief and scribbled:

babies don't actually change

Ramzi was picking muslin cloths and bits of cotton wool off the lounge carpet when Dad came in through the front door.

"*ASSALEMU ALEIKUM,* " shouted Dad.

Ramzi rushed over to the hall. "Sshhhhh. They've only just gone to sleep."

A broad grin spread across Dad's face. "Ahaaaa," he said, "with every difficulty comes relief! Now, my little warrior, tell me what you've been doing." He put his arm around Ramzi's shoulders and steered him into the kitchen.

"Well," began Ramzi, "loads of stuff. Shaima's got this totally cool aunt and she's an insectologist and studies beetles and stuff and she's got this really cool bag full of stuff and this totally rare beetle went up her arm when she was getting the pawn out of Iqbal's nose and..."

Dad raised his eyebrows. "Getting the *what* out of *where*?" he asked. But before Ramzi had time to answer, there was a noise from the lounge.

"WAAAAAAAAAAAAAAH!"

"Sorry, Ramzi," said Dad, "you'll have to tell me later." He hurried into the lounge, picked up Baby Zed and crept back to the kitchen. Pressed against Dad's warm shoulder, Baby Zed went suddenly quiet. Dad started to sing a strange wordless lullaby:

"*La, la laaaa, la laaa, la laaaa.*"

It sounded funny.

"Dad, you still haven't taken your jacket off. It's covered in baby dribble," grinned Ramzi.

"That's OK," smiled Dad. "It's a blessing."

Steaming Open the Inbox

"QUICK! Ramzi, quick – we've got mail!" yelled Shaima. Her tiny head was poking out of the door of Number Twelve.

Ramzi ran down the path, yanked off his trainers and followed Shaima into Mr Stalk's study. To his surprise, a little old woman wrapped in a chocolate-coloured shawl was sitting at the laptop.

"A... a... *assalemu aleikum*, Nanna Stalk," stammered Ramzi.

"*Wa'aleikum assalem*," she replied, spinning round on the office chair. Nanna Stalk's face was smaller than Shaima's but her glasses were just the same, only thicker.

"I told Nanna all about the website," grinned Shaima.

"What?" gulped Ramzi.

Nanna Stalk beckoned Ramzi to join her. "Don't worry. I'm not angry. Not at all. In fact, it's a wonderful idea. So glad you could join us. It's just what we need – a man's perspective. You can help us choose."

Ramzi blushed. "Choose what?" he asked.

"Choose a husband. For Aunty Urooj," grinned Shaima.

"Perhaps you should let her choose her own husband!" shouted a voice from the kitchen. It was Mrs Stalk.

"Well, she hasn't found one yet, " yelled Nanna Stalk.

"Sit down," said Shaima, pushing Ramzi on to a chair.

Ramzi cringed. He hated this sort of thing – weddings and stuff. It was so, well, *embarrassing*. He tried *not* to look at the *Truly Deeply Muslims* homepage but the flashing red love-heart kept catching his eye.

"Was this *your* idea, Ramzi?" asked Mrs Stalk, throwing her oven gloves on the desk.

"No!" said Ramzi, shaking his head. "Actually, Mrs Stalk, I think I better go. Baby Zed's not been sleeping and..."

"You *can't* go now!" said Shaima. "I'm just about to open the inbox."

Ramzi watched her tiny fingers as they logged in.

"Hurry! Hurry!" said Nanna Stalk excitedly.

"*Astaghfirullah.* What *have* you two done?" sighed Mrs Stalk.

"But Aunty Urooj wants to, Mum. Honest. Doesn't she, Ramzi?" said Shaima.

"Ramzi?" Mrs Stalk grabbed him by the shoulders and looked into his eyes. "Did Urooj actually tell you that she wants you to find her a husband?"

Ramzi's cheeks began to burn. "No... I mean... not exactly." Shaima pinched him. "*Ouch*!... She just sort of said... that she was a bit lonely. That's all."

"There. See. I told you this was all nonsense," huffed Mrs Stalk.

"Nonsense?" cried Nanna Stalk. "NONSENSE? That's fine for you to say – married to my son – with three children of your own! But think of my daughters – Zakiya and Urooj – all alone in the world. What will happen to them *when I'm gone*?"

"Don't talk like that, *Ammi*," said Mrs Stalk. "*Insha'Allah,* you'll be given a long life."

"*Insha'Allah.* But I might be gone tomorrow. Each day's a blessing – what with my sugar levels. There's no point sticking your feet in the sand, Amira."

"Head, Nanna," said Shaima. "It's 'head in the sand'."

"That's what I said, young lady. And remember..."

She waggled her finger. "I've been here a lot longer than you."

"Sorry, Nanna," said Shaima.

Mrs Stalk put her arm around Nanna Stalk's tiny shoulders. "*Ammi,* I'm sorry too. You do whatever you think is best. Now, I better get on with the cooking. Mustafa's expecting bhajis." Mrs Stalk picked up the oven gloves and hurried back into the kitchen.

Ramzi looked at his watch and got up to leave. "My mum'll be wondering..."

"You're not going anywhere," scowled Shaima.

Ramzi sat back down.

"Now, tell me, Shaima. How many letters are there?" asked Nanna Stalk, squinting at the screen.

"Five," said Shaima. She hovered the cursor over the inbox.

"*Five!*" exclaimed Nanna Stalk. "*Subhan'Allah*! This is better than Pakistan. What are we waiting for? Quick! Steam them open."

***

They all agreed. Yusef was too short. Irfan was too
fat. Suleiman was too silly. And Adam was a show-
off. Which left Rasheed: the '*Earnest entrepreneur
seeking clever and dynamic career woman for marriage
and life-time spiritual companionship.*'

"Perfect," said Nanna Stalk. "Shaima – write him
an invitation. He must bring his parents, of course.
Ask them round on Friday evening."

"What – here? At Cinnamon Grove?" asked
Shaima, typing as fast as she could.

35

"Of course *here*," replied Nanna Stalk. "Your Aunty Urooj is coming anyway, so there's no need to invite her. And your father has Friday off." Suddenly, a look of worry spread across Nanna Stalk's face. "If we were at home," she sighed, "we'd know about his family. His reputation."

"We *are* at home, Nanna," said Shaima.

Nanna sighed again. How she missed the taste of fresh mangos and the sound of chickens scratching in the yard. "But how will we know he's from a good background?" she said. "How can we check he's of *good character*?" She chewed on the arm of her spectacles while they all tried to think.

"*Monopoly!*" cried Shaima at last.

"What?" asked Ramzi, puzzled.

Shaima nodded until her plaits shook.

"*Monopoly*?" exclaimed Nanna Stalk. "Is that the best you can do? We need to find out if he's a good Muslim – with a sound job and a respectable reputation. And *you* want to know if he's talented at party games!"

"But you don't understand, Nanna," said Shaima. "I was reading this book called *The Psychology of Board Games* – and recent research suggests that games are a great way of making people reveal their 'true selves'. *Monopoly* would be perfect."

"And why would that be?" asked Nanna Stalk, still unsure.

"It's simple. Greedy people will buy up *everything*. Lazy people won't 'pass go'. Clever people will buy the utilities and..."

"And if he's not a 'good Muslim'," giggled Ramzi, "he'll keep getting 'stuck in jail'."

"That is *so* not funny," said Shaima.

They both looked at Nanna Stalk.

"Well... I don't have any better ideas," she said, "and time *is* running out. After all, your Aunty's nearly thirty-one! *Monopoly* it is. Now, let's post the invitation. I'll go and get a stamp." Nanna Stalk bustled into the hall to fetch her handbag.

Meanwhile, Shaima winked at Ramzi and pressed

SEND.

The Larval Stage

Aunty Urooj was blissfully unaware of the goings-on at Number Twelve. Whilst Shaima and Nanna Stalk were checking the inbox (one last time before bed), Aunty Urooj was staring down a microscope in her university laboratory. A curious-looking beetle was waving its unwieldy antennae under her lens.

"Excellent," said Aunty Urooj, jotting something down. Then, very carefully, she put Gulliver on to the back of her hand and let him down into a large glass tank in the corner of the room. It was packed tight with dank earth and dead wood.

Gulliver scuttled behind a rotten branch and disappeared from sight.

As she watched him go, Aunty Urooj caught sight of herself in the reflection of the glass. She smiled. Yes. The bright red headscarf went perfectly with her white overcoat and laboratory glasses.

She went over to her desk and picked up a clipboard and a bag of sticks and leaves. Then she began walking round the laboratory. It was full of glass containers – some misted up with condensation, others dry and crystal bright. There were mini-deserts and micro-jungles, cold forests and steamy swamps – all lovingly prepared. For although her work centred on British beetles, Aunty Urooj's collection came from all over the world.

The larvae would arrive in boxes bursting with bubble-wrap and stamp-marked with mysterious sounding names: *Burkina Faso ... Eritrea ... Kyrgysztan*. Fingers trembling with excitement, Aunty Urooj would open the packages and help the unborn beetles thrive in their newly-made homes.

This evening, like every other evening, Aunty Urooj was doing her nightly check. She increased the humidity level for one beetle and popped a willow leaf in for another. It usually took about forty-five minutes. But tonight it was taking longer. For tonight wasn't just any night. Something was about to happen – at least, she hoped it was. If her calculations were correct, a Rhinoceros Beetle from South America was due to emerge from its larva!

Aunty Urooj's shoulders were tense with anticipation. She checked the thermometer one last time. Perfect. She glanced at the label on the container.

Dr Stalk –
Please be careful with this rare and ENORMOUS rhinoceros beetle. Great trouble was taken to get it to you. But we feel safe in the knowledge that it is now part of the best living beetle collection in the world.

Pressing her face against the glass, Aunty Urooj peered in. Still no sign. She sighed and looked out of the window. It was getting late. Putting her clipboard back on the desk, she took off her white laboratory coat and hung it on a peg. Then she picked up her carpet bag, turned off the lights and opened the door. A yellow post-it note flapped on the glass. It said:

Aunty Urooj peeled off the note and stuffed it into her trouser pocket.

"*Insha'Allah*, your journey will be easy," she said to the dark laboratory. "Sleep tight, Gulliver."

There was a faint rustle of leaves as the door clicked shut.

When Iqbal Completely Forgot

The following evening, the Stalk family came round to coo over Baby Zed.

"I've knitted her something to keep her warm," said Nanna Stalk. She pulled a pink cardigan out of her bag and passed it to Mum. "Why don't you put the heating on, Ruby? The baby will catch cold."

Mum smiled uncertainly.

"It's *summer*," giggled Shaima. "We're the only ones in Cinnamon Grove with the heating still on."

"Summer? You can't call this summer!" exclaimed Nanna Stalk.

Mum laughed and held the cardigan in the air.

"It's perfect," she smiled, "*Jazak Allah kheir.*"

Mr Stalk was on the other side of the lounge, talking in whispers with Dad.

"It's true," sighed Mr Stalk, "my sister *is* tired of being on her own. And marriage *is* half of our religion. But is it right to interfere in these things? And in such a manner?" He rubbed his long fuzzy beard.

"Well, *brother*," said Dad, patting Mr Stalk on the shoulder, "if *you* don't find her a husband, who will?"

Mr Stalk nodded. "Yes. But *Truly Deeply Muslims Online Marriage Services*? Does it sound *halal* to you?"

Dad shrugged. "Well, as long as you follow Islamic guidelines, I don't see why it shouldn't be." He walked Mr Stalk over to the window. "We Muslims must move with the times, Mustafa. We can't rely on family connections here. We have to do things for ourselves. Look at me," he glanced at Mum, "I found myself a jewel."

Mr Stalk smiled nervously. "So you think we should meet him, then? This Rasheed Khan – the 'earnest entrepreneur'?"

"Why not?" beamed Dad. "Especially if Urooj is happy with the idea.

Nanna Stalk fidgeted on the sofa.

"*Ammi,* you have told her, haven't you?" said Mr Stalk.

"I will," said Nanna Stalk, whipping her knitting needles out of her bag.

Mr Stalk's jaw dropped open. "*Ammi*! How... could..." he stammered.

"Don't worry," said Dad. "If it's not written, it won't happen. When are you meeting him?"

"Tomorrow," said Nanna Stalk.

"Tomorrow!" exclaimed Mr Stalk. "But..."

"Look," said Nanna Stalk, glancing at the clock, "it's time for *Asr* prayers. Mustafa, stop chatting."

***

Everyone lined up on the brightly coloured prayer mats just waiting to begin. Even Baby Zed joined in. Mum had strapped her into the sling.

"Come on, Iqbal," said Ramzi. "You can stand by me."

"Iqbal not weady," said Iqbal. He was trying to

touch his nose with his tongue whilst balancing Mr Stalk's car keys on his chin.

"Iqbal," said Dad kindly, "you're a big boy now, *masha'Allah*. When you do *salat,* you should try to forget about the things of this world."

Iqbal ran into the kitchen.

"Now where's he gone?" asked Mr Stalk. Mrs Stalk, Nanna Stalk, Shaima and Mum all shuffled into their line.

"Go and get him, Ramzi, we'll wait," smiled Dad.

Iqbal was raiding the fruit bowl in the kitchen, his mouth stuffed full of grapes. Ramzi dragged him back to the lounge and did the *iqama*. Iqbal stood very still with his hands cupped behind his ears – copying Ramzi. Then everyone began their *rakats*: heads bobbing up and down in neat little rows. Iqbal did quite well at first. But then he saw a black cat on the window ledge and raced over to stroke the glass.

"Hello puddy cat. Iqbal pwaying," he said.

With foreheads pressed against soft prayer mats, no one said a word. But the room filled with silent smiles.

When everyone had finished their prayers, Dad asked the Stalks to stay for dinner.

"I'll make you *boureks*," he said.

"Don't go to any trouble," said Mrs Stalk.

"Trouble? What trouble? Days like this are a bounty from the Creator," said Dad cheerfully, stroking Baby Zed's hair.

Mr Stalk smiled. "Perhaps, brother, you could teach me how to make these *boureks*? I could put them on the menu at *The Spice Pot.*"

Dad rubbed his hands together and beamed. "A Pakistani restaurant with an Algerian twist. Classic. How long have we got?"

Mr Stalk looked at his watch: "Well ... I've left

Abdullah in charge until 9pm. Plenty of time."

"But Ruby," said Mrs Stalk. "Think of all the dirty dishes."

"Don't be silly," said Mum, "Mohamed's right – we just need a bit more cumin and cheese."

"Your wish is my command," grinned Dad, taking a little bow. "Brother, let's fetch the supplies."

"Iqbal coming too?" asked Iqbal.

"And us?" chimed Shaima and Ramzi.

"Of course. Get in the car." Dad took Baby Zed out of Mum's sling and squeezed her into her tiny cardigan. She looked like a doll.

"Why don't you leave Baby Zed with us?" said Mum.

"Why?" asked Dad, surprised

"Because she's six weeks old. And three children *and* a baby is a bit of a handful," said Mum.

Dad laughed. "She thinks we can't manage it, brother. Now, where are my keys? I'm sure I left them in here somewhere." Dad looked on the shelf above the fireplace.

"I don't even know," announced Iqbal proudly.

Dad turned round.

"But you were playing with them, Iqbal," said Shaima. "Where did you put them?"

Iqbal shrugged and grinned.

"*Iqbal*," said Mrs Stalk, "Tell Mr Ramadan where you've put his keys."

"I have completely forgot," said Iqbal.

Mr Stalk folded his arms. "Where are they, son?" he asked.

"I forgot, *Baba*. Just like Mr Wamadan told me to."

Dad laughed, pointing at Iqbal. "He's right! I did! I told him to 'forget about the things of this world'!" Dad patted Iqbal on the head. "You have another Stalk genius in the making!"

While the others were searching for the keys, Shaima worked it out. It was simple. Iqbal's fingers were sticky. He'd been eating grapes before prayers. They must be in the fruit bowl. She sauntered into the kitchen, dug about beneath the bananas and passed them to Mr Stalk.

"Excellent, Shaima. Well done," he said, waving the keys at Dad. Shaima smiled and they all bundled into the car.

The front door slammed shut. Silence.

Mum sighed. "Just listen to that... not a sound. Shall we have a cup of tea before they get back? I've got lemongrass, chamomile, mint..."

"PG Tips – strong with three sugars," said Nanna Stalk.

Mrs Stalk touched her arm. "*Ammi,* remember your sugar levels."

"And some condensed milk, please," added Nanna Stalk.

Mum laughed. "I think you're in luck," she said, digging about in the cupboard. "Now, tell me, what *were* those men talking about? For a moment I thought I heard the words: *online marriage services.*"

Rasheed Khan Passes GO

It was Friday afternoon and the Stalks' house was spotless. A faint smell of vinegar lingered in the air.

"HE'S COMING!" yelled Shaima from the upstairs window.

Mrs Stalk sprayed some rosewater in the hall, Shaima grabbed her notebook and Nanna Stalk made *dua* in the lounge.

DRRRRRIIINNG went the doorbell.

When Mr Stalk opened the door, all he saw was a huge bunch of flowers.

"*Assalemu aleikum,*" said a deep sugary voice.

"*Wa'aleikum assalem,*" replied Mr Stalk. He tried to peer over the top. "You must be..."

"That's right," said the flowers. "Rasheed Khan, at your service, sir." A hand shot out through the leaves.

Mr Stalk shook the hand and stared at the bright blue petals. It didn't feel right, inviting a bunch of flowers into the house.

"Let him in, let him in," ordered Nanna Stalk, pushing Mr Stalk aside. "What beautiful orchids – such an unusual colour – I'll put them in a vase." As she grabbed the bouquet, a gasp escaped her lips. *"Masha'Allah!"* she said. "You're not what we were expecting."

For Rasheed Khan looked like a Bollywood film star! With swept-back hair, a white cotton suit and deep brown eyes, he flashed his perfect smile. "Sorry," he said. "My profile picture wasn't very good. But it's great to meet you. You must be Urooj's big sister?"

Nanna Stalk tightened her chocolate-brown head-scarf. "I'm her mother, of course," she blushed.

Mr Stalk made a strange noise – a sort of half-laugh, half-sniff. "Apologies, it's the orchids," he sniggered.

"Take no notice of my son," said Nanna Stalk. "He's always been prone to allergies. Ever since he was a baby. Comes out in a terrible rash."

"*Ammi!*" Mr Stalk was embarrassed. "He doesn't want to know about *that.*"

Rasheed flashed another smile. Then he slipped off his white suede shoes and followed Nanna Stalk down the hall.

***

Aunty Urooj was waiting in the lounge. "*This is a complete nightmare,*" she whispered to Shaima. "*What were you and Ramzi thinking?*"

"We were just trying to help," grinned Shaima sheepishly.

"Well, I wish you wouldn't. And why on earth do we have to play *Monopoly?*"

"Well, recent research..." began Shaima.

"Forget I asked," hissed Aunty Urooj.

Rasheed swept into the room and gave his

salaams. Urooj looked at the floor and prayed it would swallow her up.

"Couldn't your parents join us?" asked Mr Stalk. "It's not really customary to come alone."

"I'm afraid they're no longer with us," sighed Rasheed, glancing upwards.

"Why is your mummy upstairs?" asked Iqbal.

"*Quiet, Iqbal,*" said Mr Stalk. "May Allah take care of them."

Nanna Stalk passed Rasheed a box of tissues. His deep brown eyes were glistening with tears. "It's not easy... being an orphan," he sniffed.

Aunty Urooj looked up. Rasheed flashed his glistening smile.

"Do sit down," said Mr Stalk, pointing to the armchair on the far side of the room. But Rasheed ignored him and sat down right opposite Aunty Urooj. Mr Stalk rubbed his beard. Things were not going as planned.

"My wife is making us some tea," he said, staring at his sister. "Why don't you go and help her."

"OK," said Aunty Urooj, taking the hint. She stood up and left the room. Mr Stalk breathed a sigh of relief until he noticed Rasheed following her with his eyes. There was an awkward silence.

"I understand that Urooj is a *doctor*?" said Rasheed.

Mr Stalk looked puzzled. *How did he know*?

"I put it on her profile," said Shaima, guessing her father's thoughts.

"What else did you put?" asked Mr Stalk.

"Oh, nothing much," said Shaima. She bit her lip. There was another awkward silence.

"Why don't you tell us a little bit about yourself?" suggested Nanna Stalk.

"It would be a pleasure," smiled Rasheed, beginning to talk.

No one noticed as Shaima began to scribble things down:

Notes on Rasheed Khan:

orphan
gives money to charity
helps old ladies cross the road
wears a flashy watch and has white
    suede shoes
says he likes animals

don't think he likes me or Iqbal

Has shiny teeth

smiles too much

Conclusion:.........something's dodgy

But Nanna Stalk seemed impressed. "So even though you're an orphan, you manage to give regularly to charity, go to the mosque *every* Friday, and always help the elderly?"

"Of course," smiled Rasheed. "I try to do as many good deeds as I can."

Shaima closed her notebook SHUT.

"What's that?" asked Rasheed.

"Oh. Nothing," said Shaima.

"No, really, what is it?" asked Rasheed. "Show me." He reached for the book.

"No!" said Shaima, stuffing it behind her back. "It's just stuff, you wouldn't be interested."

Rasheed narrowed his eyes.

"Don't worry," smiled Mr Stalk. "My daughter writes everything down. She doesn't like to miss a thing."

Suddenly Rasheed felt very warm. In fact, if it hadn't been summer, he'd have sworn the radiators were on. Perhaps this wasn't such a good idea. Maybe he should have stayed at home. He looked towards the door.

"Right," said Nanna Stalk, pulling the *Monopoly* board from under the coffee table. "I think it's time we played a little game."

"But..." began Rasheed.

"Great idea, Nanna," grinned Shaima, rolling the dice. "Double six to start!"

***

Half an hour passed and something didn't add up. No. Really. Something *didn't* add up. Shaima was the Banker and there was *no way* that Rasheed Khan could have bought Mayfair, Pall Mall, eight hotels, *all* the utilities *and* still have £1,800. It was impossible. She went through the game in her head again – counting the number of times he'd passed go, collected rent, and purchased properties. No. There was only one explanation. Rasheed – the 'enterprising entrepreneur' – had been *stealing from the Monopoly bank*! Shaima stared at him fiercely.

"Shaima – are you ill?" asked Mrs Stalk.

Shaima shook her head and threw the dice again. But she threw too hard. They bounced on to the carpet and under the chair. Everybody looked to see where they'd gone. Everyone apart from Rasheed, that is. Out of the corner of her eye, she noticed his spidery fingers grab a fistful of notes and stuff them up his sleeve! Shaima gasped.

"Is it indigestion?" asked Mrs Stalk. "I knew I'd put too much chilli in..."

"No, *Ammi*, it's not that," said Shaima.

"Perhaps she's not used to losing?" said Rasheed. "It must be hard for a girl like her."

Shaima scowled at him until her glasses slipped down her nose.

"Well, I suppose Shaima does *usually* win," said Nanna Stalk. "But I'm sure she's happy for you to be the new champion. You don't mind, do you Shaima?"

Shaima couldn't hold it in any longer. "As a matter of fact, I do!"

"Shaima! Watch your tongue!" said Mrs Stalk.

"But I saw him. He was *cheating*. He stole from the *Monopoly* Bank!"

"Cheating?" exclaimed Rasheed, horrified.

"Shaima, how could you be so rude to our guest?" said Mrs Stalk.

"*But it's true*. He just stuffed loads of money up his sleeve. And according to a recent psychological study of board games, that means..."

"I can assure you, Mr Stalk. I have never cheated in my life," protested Rasheed.

"Roll up your sleeves," said Shaima. "Prove it!"

"Please. You don't have to," said Mr Stalk.

"No, it's fine," smiled Rasheed. Very slowly, he rolled up his shirt sleeves one by one. But there was nothing! Not a note! Shaima couldn't understand it. Where had the money gone?

"I... I... don't..." she stammered.

"I am so sorry for my daughter's behaviour," said Mr Stalk, shaking his head. "She is normally such a good girl."

"But *Baba*..."

"That's enough, Shaima. Go to your room. *Now.*"

Shaima felt awful. Mr Stalk *hardly ever* told her off. And when he did, it felt like there was a hole in the universe and she was tumbling through.

She could feel Rasheed's eyes staring at her as she walked past him. Too embarrassed to look up, she kept her head down and squeezed round the table. Past his pile of money. All £2,300 of it. She left the room and walked upstairs.

Hang on a minute.

£2,300?

But he'd only got £1,800!

So he *had* been cheating. She knew it. She was *never* wrong. She paused on the stairs. No. There was no point turning back. They wouldn't believe her. She went into her bedroom and slammed the door.

***

It was another twelve minutes and forty-two seconds before Rasheed Khan left the house. Shaima timed him on her stopwatch. Her bedroom window was wide open so she heard him walk away. He was talking on his *iphone*. At least, she *thought* she heard him:

"Stop ringing me, Mum. *I told you*, I'm working late," the voice said.

Shaima crept across her bedroom and peered out of the window to check. Cotton suit. White suede shoes. Flicked-back hair. She ducked back inside.

Yes. It was definitely Rasheed Khan. But didn't he just say 'Mum'?

"I knew it," said Shaima, gritting her teeth and grabbing her notebook. She peered back over the window ledge and watched him walk down Cinnamon Grove. Benjamin Butley's cat was just outside Ramzi's house. It padded over to Rasheed and curled its tail around his leg. Rasheed stopped. Then he shook his leg hard and sent the cat flying across the pavement!

"MEEEEOW," squealed the cat, darting into a hedge.

Shaima gasped and wrote it all down.

Rasheed swept back his hair, put on his shades and disappeared round the corner.

With her notebook as 'evidence', Shaima raced downstairs.

"Aunty Urooj, Nanna, Ammi, I've just seen Rasheed Khan kicking Benjamin Butley's cat. And he was on the phone *to his mum*."

"Shaima, what *is* the matter with you?" asked Nanna Stalk.

"It's the pressure," said Mrs Stalk. "Perhaps Shaima's not ready for the entrance exam."

"Of course I'm ready!" said Shaima.

"Then try to be nice," said Nanna Stalk. "Rasheed Khan is a good Muslim boy. He gives his money to charity, he's kind to old people *and* he takes care of his family in Pakistan. You did very well to find him."

Shaima felt a bit sick. "But..."

"Your Nanna's right," nodded Mrs Stalk. "And remember, as Muslims, it's our duty to look after the orphans."

"But he's *not* an orphan," said Shaima. "I just told you, I heard him talking to his mum."

Nanna Stalk and Mrs Stalk shook their heads and sighed.

Mr Stalk and Aunty Urooj came in from the lounge.

"*Baba...*" she said, "tell them. *Please.*"

Mr Stalk frowned. "Shaima – for the first time in my life, I was *not* proud of you today."

Shaima's heart sank. "Sorry, *Baba,*" she said.

At that moment, Shaima Stalk knew she had to do something she'd never done before. She had to *prove* that she was right. But she couldn't do it alone. She needed her best friend, Ramzi Ramadan.

The Black Cat Detectives

The following morning, Shaima and Ramzi were huddled on the doorstep of Number Twelve – talking in hushed whispers.

"But what if you're wrong about him?" asked Ramzi.

"Me? Wrong?" said Shaima.

Ramzi shrugged. She was right. Ollie was never wrong.

"It's like he's cast a spell on them all," sighed Shaima. "First he lied about being an orphan. Then he stole from the *Monopoly* Bank. And then he kicked Benjamin's Butley's cat. I'm telling you, Ramzi, he's *totally* bad news." Her glasses started to mist up.

"OK, all right, all right. I believe you," said Ramzi.

"Good," huffed Shaima. "But *they* don't believe me. Aunty Urooj is all gooey-eyed, Nanna's sighing over wedding saris, and Mum thinks I'm 'stressed' about the exam. It's *so* annoying."

"What about your dad?" asked Ramzi.

Shaima shrugged her shoulders. Some things are too hard to say.

Ramzi looked thoughtful. "What you need is proof," he said.

"I know. That's why I wanted to talk to you." She looked at him and smiled.

"Shaima," he said, "your eyes are doing that weird sparkly thing."

"What weird sparkly thing?"

"You know, when you're having a brainwave or whatever."

"Well," said Shaima, slowly. "I was just thinking that we could set up our own Detective Agency."

"A Detective Agency? In Cinnamon Grove?" Ramzi grinned. This was why his best friend was a girl – Benjamin Butley never had ideas like this.

"I've got a secret casebook already," said Shaima. "Aunty Zakiya gave it to me for *Eid*." Checking that no one was around, she grabbed her bag from the hall. Ramzi watched as she pulled out a beautiful, red leather notebook. The padlock glinted in the sun.

"That is soooo cool!" said Ramzi. "But what are we going to call it?"

"What?" asked Shaima.

"The Detective Agency, of course."

Shaima chewed her lip as they both looked around for inspiration.

A postman whizzed past on his bicycle and waved at them. They waved back.

"Post box... red letter box... the red letter... the scarlet letter..." murmured Shaima. "No...."

Mrs Butterworth, the cheery lollipop lady from Number Three, came jogging out of the alleyway.

"The Sweaty Joggers... the Secret Legwarmer... the Lollipop Spies... oh, I've got it: The Runaway Detective Agency," said Ramzi.

Shaima crinkled up her nose. "I dunno. It's not very... catchy."

Ramzi sighed. Shaima was *not* an easy girl to please.

Just then, Benjamin Butley's cat came shimmying past, its long black tail waving in the air. They looked at each other and grinned. *"The Black Cat Detective Agency,"* they both said at once.

"And we'll need some secret agent stuff," said Ramzi.

"Like what?" asked Shaima. She hadn't thought about that.

"Like a telescope, and some pens with invisible ink, and a magnifying glass, and some walkie talkies and..."

"We're going to Aunty Zakiya's on Saturday –

on the way back from the Open Day. She's got loads of old stuff. Why don't you come?"

"What Open Day?" asked Ramzi.

"At *Greystone's Academy for the Bright and Gifted*," said Shaima.

"Oh," said Ramzi, frowning. He didn't want Shaima to go to a different school.

"*Please*, Ramzi. I need your help. You've got to come," said Shaima.

"OK," said Ramzi. "I'll ask Mum."

Shaima sighed with relief. It was going to be all right after all. *The Black Cat Detective Agency* would save the day and no one would break Aunty Urooj's lonely beetle-loving heart!

Ramzi Wins a Prize

Greystone's Academy for the Bright and Gifted was so old it smelt of the past. According to Shaima, it was an Elizabethan mansion, but Ramzi thought it looked more like a ghost ride. It had turrets, and doorways and arches – and was surrounded by enormous, tall trees. Mrs Stalk parked the mud-splattered people-carrier on the gravel and they walked up the long, winding drive.

"*Ammi*," cried Iqbal, clutching his trousers, "*I'm desperate.*"

"I told you to go before we left the house," said Mrs Stalk.

"I did," said Iqbal. "But it didn't work."

Mrs Stalk grabbed his arm and hurried over to the woman greeting visitors.

"Excuse me," asked Mrs Stalk, "could you please advise us as to where the conveniences are?"

"Why's your mum speaking like the Queen?" whispered Ramzi.

"She's not!" snapped Shaima.

The woman led them up the steps and pointed down a corridor. "Just follow the signs to Year Eight's horticultural display and it's on your left."

"You have been too kind. Many thanks," smiled Mrs Stalk.

"Did your mum just curtsey then?" asked Ramzi.

"Of course not," growled Shaima.

"*Ammi*," cried Iqbal, twisting his legs. Mrs Stalk picked up the hem of her *jilbab* and raced down the corridor, Iqbal swinging along at her side.

Nanna Stalk, Shaima and Ramzi looked at the

woman. The woman fiddled with her pearls and tried to think of something to say.

"So you must be Amin's family?" she said at last. "How terribly nice to meet you."

Nanna Stalk eyed her suspiciously and nodded her head. When the woman's back was turned, Nanna Stalk whispered to Shaima: "How did she know?"

"Know what?" asked Shaima.

"That we're Amin's family, of course!" hissed Nanna Stalk. She straightened the creases in her *jilbab* and clutched her bag of samosas to her chest.

"Just a lucky guess, I s'pose," grinned Ramzi.

***

The pupils at *The Academy* were a different species. Tall girls wearing long tartan skirts glided around the Grand Hall while serious boys in blazers gave out cups of tea by the door. Ramzi wished he wasn't wearing a skateboard top and jeans. He tried to flatten down his curls but they kept bouncing back.

"You look cool," laughed Shaima.

"It's all right for you," said Ramzi.

Shaima was wearing a dark green pinafore with matching bows in her hair. But Ramzi wasn't even wearing matching socks. Mum used to wrap them into neat little balls and put them in his wardrobe, but since Baby Zed was born, his sock drawer had been empty.

"Hey, there's Amin!" Shaima was pointing to the stage at the far end of the hall. "Come on." They pushed their way past a mini-chess tournament, a fancy cake stall and a blindfolded boy trying to 'pin the tail on the asteroid'.

"Amin! *Salem!*" called Shaima as she clambered up on to the stage. Ramzi followed.

"*Salem*, guys," smiled Amin. He wore cool glasses

and an easy smile. "Long time no see, little sis. Ramzi – good to see you here. Thinking of applying?" Ramzi shook his head.

"You should," said Shaima. "Those maps you draw are awesome. And you know the capital city of everywhere!" Ramzi blushed. "Go on, try him," said Shaima.

Amin leant against the table. "OK... What's the capital of the Kingdom of Bhutan?" Shaima stared at Ramzi, expectant.

"Thimphu," he said, effortlessly.

"Population size?" asked Amin.

"According to the UN, about 708,500," said Ramzi.

"Current Head of State?" continued Amin.

"King Jigme Khesar Namgyel Wangchuck, but it's hardly like I'm anything special," said Ramzi.

"No way. You should *definitely* apply. That's awesome."

Ramzi laughed. "I'm only good at maps and stuff."

"Yeh, right," smiled Shaima.

"Whatever," shrugged Amin. "Why don't you have a go at the 'Sweet Jar Guesstimate'?" he said, pointing to the jar on the table. "There's a totally random prize."

Shaima folded her arms and stared at the jar. "Well," she began, "if the volume of the jar is the height times the surface of the base." Her mind began to whizz like a noisy hard drive. "And if the sweet is about

3 cm^3, then the number of sweets is... 53 x 100 π ÷ 3... approximately... 5546."

"Not bad, little sis," grinned Amin, writing her answer down. "Your turn, Ramzi."

Ramzi gulped. "No thanks. I told you... I can only do maps and stuff."

"Go on," said Shaima. "Have a go."

Ramzi looked at the sweets. There were loads. But he couldn't write that. He looked at the column of answers. They were all similar. He picked a number somewhere in the middle: "5,777," he said at last. "But it's just a guess."

"Cool," said Amin, scribbling the answer down. "And take no notice of Shaima. She's not exactly *normal*." He winked.

"What's so good about *normal*, anyway?" said Shaima, digging Amin in the ribs.

A loud voice echoed through the speakers at the back of the stage:

"Could all those wishing to have a guided tour, please come to the refectory?"

"That's the new Deputy Head," said Amin. "Professor Entwistle."

"Where's the Headmistress?" asked Shaima, clearly disappointed. "Has she left?"

"No. She's in Geneva .... taking the sixth form to visit to the Hadron Collider."

"You mean that huge tunnel where they collide particle-beams at super-fast speeds?" asked Shaima.

Ramzi tried to picture it: a sort of underground motorway full of flashing torch lights and bouncing dots.

"What are they doing that for?" he asked.

"So they can understand the origins of matter immediately after the Big Bang," said Amin. "You know, they're sort of like trying to understand 'the mind of God'."

"I *so* want to come to this school!" grinned Shaima. Then she remembered something and her face fell. "Amin, I really need to talk to you," she said.

"Why? What's up? What've you done?"

"Well..." Shaima fiddled with one of her plaits. "It's not me, *exactly*. It's Aunty Urooj. I'm really worried about her and it's kind of all my fault."

***

A few words can change everything. One minute, Shaima felt awful. But the next minute, she was on cloud nine. For Amin *loved* the idea of *The Black Cat Detective Agency* and he was *sure* that Ramzi and Shaima would get to the bottom of the mystery of Rasheed Khan.

Sometimes that's all you need: someone who believes in you. Shaima gave Amin a big hug and breathed a sigh of relief. He hugged her back and patted her head.

"Hey, there's your Nanna," said Ramzi, pointing at the crowd. Nanna Stalk was waving a plastic bag in the air.

"*Alhamdulillah* – she's brought me some 'real' food at last," grinned Amin. He leapt across the table and down off the stage.

"What's wrong with the food here?" asked Ramzi.

"Not *halal*," shouted Amin. "And if I have to eat another lentil bake, I'm going to..."

"Lentils are a fantastic source of iron and..." began Shaima.

"Shaima... I love ya... but give it a rest," yelled Amin.

Shaima grinned at Ramzi and they chased after Amin, squeezing their way through the crowd. When they reached him, Amin was throwing Iqbal in the air, making him squeal with laughter.

"Look what we've brought you," smiled Nanna Stalk, opening her supermarket bag.

Amin put his head inside and took a deep breath. "Ahhhhh! Home!" he sighed.

"Not home, silly," giggled Iqbal. "It's *samosas*."

***

Ramzi and Shaima had never seen anything like it. They watched gunpowder experiments in the science block, heard didgeridoo recitals in the music rooms, and watched the Maths teacher do handstands on his desk!

"Mr Braithwaite says it helps him think," grinned Amin. Ramzi and Shaima laughed. "Come on, or we'll miss the Prize-giving Ceremony."

They rushed back to the Grand Hall and found the others, just in time. Certificates had already been given out for *Mathematical Chairs*, *Pin the Tail on the Asteroid* and *Latin Whispers*.

"And now for the *Sweet Jar Guesstimate*," said Professor Entwistle. "It gives me great pleasure to tell you that the winner is...." There was a deep hush as the professor opened the envelope. "... Mr Ramzi Ramadan."

Nanna Stalk clapped loudly but Ramzi blushed. "I just copied everyone else," he whispered to Shaima.

"But *your* guess was right."

"Really?" asked Ramzi. "You mean, you don't mind?"

"'Course not!" said Shaima.

She nudged him with her arm and Ramzi stumbled through the crowd. With churning stomach and shaking knees, he staggered up to the stage.

"*Assalemu aleikum*, Ramzi, well done," said Professor Entwistle, shaking Ramzi's hand. Ramzi looked up at the Professor and felt his cheeks burn. Stooping over, the Professor spoke into the microphone:

"Congratulations – and this year's prize is..." He opened a blue envelope: "A hot air balloon ride for four! Courtesy of *The Pendragon Balloon Company*!"

The hall echoed with applause as Professor Entwistle gave Ramzi the tickets.

Ramzi was lost for words. A hot air balloon ride! He'd *always* wanted to go up in a hot air balloon. And four tickets meant that he could take

Shaima – suddenly he didn't feel so bad. He turned and grinned at the sea of clapping hands.

***

"Who are you going to take?" asked Amin, making space for Ramzi in the crowd.

"You and Shaima, of course. Oh, and my dad," said Ramzi.

"What about your mum?" asked Amin.

"She's got Baby Zed."

"Great!" grinned Amin.

But Ramzi was looking thoughtful. "How come Professor Entwistle gave me *salaams*?" he asked.

"Because your name's '*Ramadan*', you muppet," laughed Shaima.

"No ... but ... I mean, he said it *perfectly*."

"'Cos he's Muslim," said Amin.

"Really?" said Ramzi.

"Muslim?" blinked Shaima, staring at the stage. Professor Entwistle was giving a hamper of pickles to the winner of the chess tournament. "He *can't* be Muslim."

"Why not?" asked Amin.

"Well..." began Shaima.

79

"It's cos he hasn't got a beard, isn't it?" interrupted Ramzi.

"No!" said Shaima. "Of course not." She looked at Professor Entwistle's sparkling blue eyes and neatly trimmed blonde moustache. "It's just that..." Her voice trailed off.

The professor continued: "*And now, I am delighted to announce the winner of the grand raffle....*"

"It's cos he's English, then," said Ramzi. "I bet you don't think *I* look very Muslim either. Well, let me remind you, Shaima Stalk, the Prophet Muhamed (peace be upon him) wasn't actually from Pakistan."

"Sorry," stammered Shaima, "I didn't mean..."

But Shaima Stalk was lost for words. Ramzi noticed that her bottom lip was quivering.

He looked at Professor Entwistle again and felt bad. He couldn't really blame her. With his dark green cords, tweed blazer and gingham shirt, Professor Entwistle looked like he was going to a fox hunt, not a mosque.

"Forget it," said Ramzi. "It doesn't matter. Honest."

"Are we still partners?" asked Shaima anxiously.

"Yeh – 'course, Agent Stalk."

Shaima smiled.

"Will you two stop your chattering!" said Nanna Stalk, putting her finger to her lips. "I want to see if I won the *Rubix Cube Contest.*"

Cash in the Attic

Nanna Stalk was gracious in defeat. "Well, I can't expect to win everything. Not at my age," she said. "Especially when most of those children have the brains of elephants."

"Do they?" asked Iqbal, surprised.

Ramzi leant as far forward as his seatbelt would let him. "I didn't know elephants were clever," he said.

"Oh yes," nodded Nanna Stalk. "They've always struck me as being most wise."

"We're here," said Mrs Stalk, pulling the hand break on the people-carrier. "Belts off."

"Nanna..." began Iqbal, "can I be an elephant when I grow up?"

"You're a bit of a Dumbo already," giggled Shaima.

"Shaima! Manners," said Mrs Stalk.

Iqbal leapt out of the car, opened an old wooden gate and raced down Aunty Zakiya's garden path, swinging his trunk as he went.

"And this," said Shaima, waving her hand, "is Aunty Zakiya's cottage."

It had yellow roses trailing over the front door and apple trees in the garden. Ramzi thought it looked like one of those cottages on fancy biscuit tins. At least, he did at first. But then he noticed something strange. There were cardboard boxes and bubble wrap pressed against the downstairs windows.

"Is she moving house?" asked Ramzi.

"No," smiled Shaima, "I told you – she collects things."

Rat a tat tat.

The brass knocker clattered and the curtains twitched. Then, after what seemed like forever, someone opened the door. Ramzi guessed it was Aunty Zakiya but he couldn't be sure. You see, the person in front of him looked like a black pillar-box – with the slit for the letters framing sparkly brown eyes.

"Whyever are you wearing *niqab*?" exclaimed Nanna Stalk. "We're just family."

Aunty Zakiya glanced at Ramzi and winked. "Not all of you," she said. "So, *this* is Ramzi Ramadan?"

"Yes. But he's *only* a child, Zakiya," said Nanna Stalk. "Really, you're taking this too far!"

"Are you Ramzi – only a child?" Aunty Zakiya's eyes twinkled mischievously.

"No," said Ramzi. "I'm nearly eleven already."

"Exactly," nodded the black pillar-box. "*Ammi,* why do you always have to be so..."

"So what?" asked Nanna Stalk.

"Well, so... old-fashioned," said Aunty Zakiya.

"Old-fashioned?" exclaimed Nanna Stalk. "For your information, young lady, I spent most of last week canoeing on the internet."

"You mean 'surfing'," said Shaima.

"That's what I said!" snapped Nanna Stalk.

Aunty Zakiya's eyes smiled. "Well done, *Ammi*," she said, kissing both her cheeks. "Now, where's my favourite nephew and niece?"

"All of me's here," grinned Iqbal, throwing himself at the black cloth. Aunty Zakiya tickled him until he wriggled with laughter.

"Aunty," said Shaima, peering into the hall. "Do you think you've got some spare magnifying glasses?"

"Are you looking for bugs again?" asked Aunty Zakiya.

"No, it's not that," said Shaima. "We're ..." She stopped and looked at Ramzi. She couldn't tell them about *The Black Cat Detective Agency*, could she?

Ramzi could see her weakening. "It's a matter of national importance," he said. "But we're sworn to total secrecy."

"I see," said Aunty Zakiya. "In that case,

you'd better see what you can find. This house is full of treasures!"

Ramzi and Shaima ran off. Meanwhile, Mrs Stalk slipped off her flip-flops and Nanna squeezed past the stacked boxes in the hall.

"When will you have enough?" asked Nanna Stalk.

"It's my job, *Ammi*. I'm an antique dealer. It's how I pay my bills. Why won't you at least try and understand?"

"Because you trained to be a lawyer, Zakiya. You could have had the world at your feet." Nanna Stalk pushed past her daughter and bustled down the hall.

"I don't want the world at my feet," sighed Aunty Zakiya, looking at her toes. "I like it exactly where it is."

"She just worries about you, that's all," said Mrs Stalk, patting Aunty Zakiya's shoulder.

"Then tell her to stop worrying. I'm fine. Now... tell me about Amin. How is he doing?"

"He's all hungry," said Iqbal, rubbing his tummy. "Iqbal hungry too."

Aunty Zakiya laughed. "Well, it's a good job I've

made cake," she said. "Come on, there's still some space to sit in the lounge."

***

"I've found something!" cried Ramzi. He was peering under a white cotton sheet behind an old chest-of-drawers. "It's much better than a magnifying glass."

"Let's see," Shaima scrambled across the room and helped pull back the sheet. And there it was – an old wooden telescope on a gleaming bronze stand.

"Awesome!" sighed Shaima. "But do you think it still works?"

"Sure," said Ramzi. He tilted the telescope in the direction of the window, up towards the sky. A distant flock of starlings lurched into view.

"Of course it works," said Aunty Zakiya, her black outline popping round the door. "I'm an antique dealer, not a rag-and-bone man. Now come and have a mango smoothie. I've put extra ice-cream in." She disappeared, the drinks tray rattling down the hall.

"It's my turn now," said Shaima, elbowing Ramzi aside. Standing on tiptoe, she lowered the telescope and swivelled it round on its stand.

"Careful!" exclaimed Ramzi. Just in time! He'd only just managed to catch the strange-looking vase that Shaima had knocked off the windowsill.

"WHATEVER YOU DO, DON'T GO NEAR THAT CHINESE VASE," called Aunty Zakiya. "IT MIGHT BE FROM THE QUAINLONG DYNASTY."

"Phew! That was close!" said Ramzi, putting the vase back.

Shaima turned to Ramzi. "Did she just say *Quainlong Dynasty?*"

"Yeh – I think so."

"*Subhan'Allah!*" exclaimed Shaima. "One of those just sold for 43 million pounds!"

"No way!" exclaimed Ramzi. They both stared at the vase. The weird fish swimming across its surface seemed to stare back at them.

"It must be a fake," said Ramzi, taking a step backwards. "I mean ... she wouldn't just leave it here if it was worth *that* much."

"Of course not," nodded Shaima. "That would be silly." But she moved the telescope away from the vase, just in case.

"Anyway," said Ramzi, turning his back on the vase. "Do you reckon this thing's good enough for *The Black Cat Detective Agency,* Agent Stalk?"

Shaima peered through the lens. "Well, I can see right into that man's car. He's eating some crisps...

they're salt and vinegar... and he's got a tattoo on his wrist. Yeh. I think it'll be great, Agent Ramadan."

Ramzi noticed a tiny red car out of the window. It was weaving its way through distant hedgerows.

"Let's have a look," said Ramzi. He peered through the telescope and the car shot into range. Sure enough, there was the crisp packet, the hand and the tattoo!

"This'd be perfect for spying with," he said. "But will she let us have it?"

Shaima just grinned.

***

It was getting late by the time they left. Nanna Stalk was strapping Iqbal into his car seat whilst Mrs Stalk was squeezing the antique telescope into the boot of the car.

"I can't believe she just *gave* it to you," said Ramzi. Shaima laughed.

"Well of course she gave it to you," sighed Nanna Stalk. "That daughter of mine has no sense of money."

Ramzi looked back at the house and saw Aunty Zakiya's pillar-box silhouette appear behind the closed curtains. Two arms stretched up as she took off her *niqab* – and a new silhouette appeared – a slight little figure with a bobbing pony tail. Then she was gone.

"Why does she live here on her own?" asked Ramzi.

"Cos she likes it," said Shaima.

"But isn't it a bit ..."

"What?"

"I dunno... spooky?"

The cottage looked eerie as it faded in the half-light. And it was *so* quiet. Not like Cinnamon Grove. At home, there was always the hum of distant traffic. A dog barking. An ice-cream van. A child laughing outside. But on the winding lane outside Aunty Zakiya's house, there was only the sound of the wind.

"We're *always* asking her to move back to Cinnamon Grove," began Mrs Stalk.

"But she's as stubborn as a mule," interrupted Nanna Stalk.

"*Nanna!*" said Shaima.

Mrs Stalk started the engine and drove down the twisting lane.

"Do you reckon there are ghosts here?" asked Ramzi, peering into the thickening darkness.

"You mean 'unexplained supernatural phenomena'?" said Shaima.

"Yeh," said Ramzi. He could feel the skin tingling on the back of his neck.

"No," said Shaima. "It's highly unlikely. You're probably just experiencing some sort of mild anxiety."

"Am not," said Ramzi. But he felt disappointed. Why did Shaima have to be so *logical* about everything? He looked up at the pale, charcoal sky and watched the stars appear – one by one. He traced them with his finger. 'I'll go up there, one day,' he thought. 'Outer Space. Beyond the Final Frontier. Where no man has gone before....'

Shaima prodded his arm. "You're doing it again, Agent Ramadan," she said.

"What?"

"Dreaming," said Shaima.

"Nothing wrong with dreaming," shouted Mrs Stalk, over the sound of the radio. "In fact, I've always thought that dreaming is what makes us human..."

"But animals dream too, *Ammi,*" said Shaima. "When four rats had micro-electrodes implanted in their hippocampus..." Suddenly, her voice became strange and muffled: "*Iqbal!* 'ill you *'lease* take your 'oot out of my 'ouf!"

Ramzi smiled in the darkness. He loved being with the Stalks. But he couldn't wait to get home. It felt like he'd been away for weeks, not just a day. He hoped Baby Zed was OK and that Mum and Dad weren't worried about him.

Something dug into his leg. He reached into his pocket and brought out a crumpled envelope – the tickets for the Hot Air Balloon Ride! How could he have forgotten? His stomach swirled with excitement. Not long now.

Don't Panic!

When Ramzi got home that night, Baby Zed was already fast asleep. It felt good to be the only one again. I mean, he loved his new little sister. But it was the first time in weeks that he'd had Mum and Dad all to himself. Dad made some warm, sweet, fluffy milk – full of sugar and cinnamon – and Mum prepared a plate of hot buttered toast. Then they sat around the kitchen table and just waited for Ramzi to talk.

Mum and Dad blinked in amazement as he described the gunpowder experiments at *The Academy*. They gasped when he told them about the nearly-smashed Chinese vase. And they clapped after he said he'd won the *Sweet Jar Guesstimate*.

But when he showed them the tickets for the *Hot Air Balloon Ride,* Dad's face fell.

"But there's *four* tickets," said Dad.

"Yeh, I know," grinned Ramzi.

"... but that means *four* people," said Dad, slowly.

Ramzi smiled. "Yeh, Dad. Me, Shaima, Amin and *you.*"

"Me?" said Dad.

"Go on!" laughed Mum. "It'll be fun."

"Fun?"

"Yeh. It'll be totally cool," said Ramzi.

"*Cool?*" said Dad, his voice rising to a squeak.

Mum nudged Ramzi. "I think Dad's just lost the power of speech," she said.

"I am p...p... perfectly c...c... capable of speech," stuttered Dad. "It is just that... well... I've got vertigo... so it's impossible for me to go up in a Hot Air Balloon. I mean... I'd love to... but... well... surfaces just *can't* be trusted."

"You can do it, Mohamed," said Mum.

"*Ruby* – vertigo is an illness, not an attitude," said Dad.

"I know, love. But remember all those cliff walks we did on our honeymoon?"

"I was a young man then – besides..." Dad blushed.

Mum skipped over and pinched his cheek. "Oh, you old dafty," she said.

"Dad, I *really* want you to come," pleaded Ramzi. "It won't be the same without you."

"Why don't you take Mum, son? She'd love it." Dad put his arm round Mum's shoulders and squeezed hard.

"Oh no," laughed Mum, shaking her head. "You're not getting away with it that easily. Besides, *someone's* got to look after Baby Zed."

"*I'll* do that," said Dad. "Not a problem. *I* can change nappies. *I* can sing songs. I could even take her swimming."

"Swimming?" said Mum, horrified. "She's six weeks old and needs feeding every two hours! There's no way I'd go gallivanting off in a hot air balloon while you drown our baby at the local pool!"

"*Dad*," pleaded Ramzi. "I *really* want you to come."

Dad winced. "*Really*?"

Ramzi nodded. "Yes!"

"Well..." said Dad, taking a deep breath. "I suppose that the believer should have *no* fear..."

Mum looked at Ramzi and winked.

"OK," said Dad. "I'll do it. But just this once."

"I knew you would," grinned Ramzi. "It's next Saturday. Half past ten. On Bartholomew's Mount."

Dad gulped and mumbled something in Arabic.

Agent Ramadan – Over and Out

Shaima was on her hands and knees – a tall glass pressed against her ear. It wasn't just any glass. It was a Black Cat Detective's spy-glass and she could hear *everything* in the room below.

"I never thought I'd learn to ice-skate! Not at my age!" laughed Nanna Stalk.

"Did you see him glide across the ice, *Ammi*?" said Aunty Urooj.

"Yes, *masha'Allah*. And such a gentleman. Helping old ladies on to the rink. What kindness. And to think that he's an orphan – with no guidance – yet such beautiful manners."

Shaima felt sick. What was wrong with them?

Why couldn't they see that Rasheed Khan was no good? She put the glass on the table next to her Black Cat Detective Casebook. Then she tiptoed over to the telescope.

"Shaima – have you finished your non-verbal, mathematically puzzling paper yet?" called Mrs Stalk.

"Nearly!" shouted Shaima. Her spectacles clattered against the lens. Suddenly Rasheed Khan was larger than life. She could see the hairs on the back of his neck! She moved the telescope to the right. A blackbird looked her in the eye. Blast. She moved it left and down a bit. Good. His hand. He was texting somebody. Probably his mum. Or maybe worse? Maybe…. Shaima grabbed the telescope off its stand, stuffed it into an old sports bag and ran downstairs.

THUD, THUD, THUD.

"Where are you going?" shouted Mrs Stalk. "I need to mark your work."

Shaima put her head round the door, plaits swinging like pendulums. "I'm just going to play football with Ramzi," she said. "Exercise stimulates the brain. I won't be long." The door slammed shut.

"But..." Mrs Stalk leaned over the sink, pressing her hand against the window, "you *hate* football."

Shaima kept on running.

"*Ammi,*" said Iqbal, pulling on Mrs Stalk's bright green sari. "Can I put these in a special place?"

Mrs Stalk turned round. Iqbal had three fat snails stuck on his arm.

"EUCH!" shrieked Mrs Stalk. "Get those things out of my kitchen!"

Aunty Urooj stroked one of the snail's shells. "They're so misunderstood, poor things. Come on, Iqbal. Why don't we go to the park and find your beautiful snails a new home?"

Iqbal grinned.

"But I thought you had a plane to catch," said Mrs Stalk. "Don't you have to be in Dusseldorf tonight?"

"There's always time to look after gastropods," smiled Aunty Urooj.

Mrs Stalk sighed in despair.

"I like you being a doctor of snails, Aunty 'Rooj," said Iqbal, as they skipped to the park.

"And I like you being Iqbal," smiled Aunty Urooj.

***

Ramzi was playing football in his garden when Shaima flew past. "Drop everything, Agent Ramadan," she yelled

He'd been hiding behind a fence when Rasheed Khan had walked by, so he was totally ready for action.

"I've got you covered, Agent Stalk," he shouted, leaping over the gate and tumble-rolling across the pavement.

"What are you doing?" hissed Shaima.

"It's what secret agents do," said Ramzi. "I saw it on TV."

Shaima blinked in disbelief. "*Not* in Cinnamon Grove. Get back in the hedge, he'll see you!"

Ramzi pressed himself against the shrubbery.

"Right. It's all clear. Let's follow," said Shaima.

The Black Cat Detectives kept at a safe distance, jumping into hedgerows or behind parked cars whenever Rasheed Khan slowed his pace.

Ramzi was beginning to get out of breath. "What are we following him for, exactly?" he asked.

"We're collecting *evidence*, of course! Quick! Hide!" Shaima grabbed Ramzi by the t-shirt and yanked him into a bush. Rasheed had stopped. A bus chugged passed, obscuring their view. It turned the corner. He was gone!

"Oh no! We've lost him!" exclaimed Ramzi. But Shaima was smiling, her hand cupped by her ear. Ramzi listened and heard a faint bell ring. It was the unmistakable sound of the door to *Café Rouge*.

"Follow him, Agent Ramadan," said Shaima.

"Why me?" asked Ramzi, brushing the leaves off his head.

"Because he knows what I look like. He's never

seen *you* – you're the perfect spy. Go on. Quick. I'll watch your back."

"You'll do *what*?" asked Ramzi, puzzled.

"It's what secret agents do," winked Shaima. "I saw it on TV." She pulled The Black Cat Detectives' telescope and the bright red casebook out of her bag. "And don't forget to take notes," she said. "Here, have this. And don't lose it." She passed Ramzi an 'invisible ink' pen. "The ink just rubs off if we need to destroy the evidence."

"Cool," said Ramzi. "Where did you get it?"

Shaima just tapped her nose. "Any problems – just make a sign."

"OK," said Ramzi, stuffing the casebook and pen up his t-shirt. "What sort of sign?"

"I don't know. Scratch your head or something. Just hurry up." Shaima pushed Ramzi out of the bushes and darted back into the leaves.

"But I haven't got any money!" hissed Ramzi. Some coins came flying out of the shrub. Ramzi was trying to catch them when he bumped into an old man walking his dog.

"Blimey!" laughed the man. "And I thought they said money doesn't grow on trees."

Ramzi forced a smile. Then he grabbed the coins as they spun on the pavement and took a deep breath. He'd never been in a café on his own before. But he wasn't going to tell Shaima that. No. He was going to pretend that this was completely normal. After all, he wasn't Ramzi Ramadan. He was *Agent* Ramadan. And he had a mission.

***

"*Driiiiiiing.*" The café bell rang loudly. Ramzi turned his face towards the window, in case he'd been seen. Then he sidled over to the counter.

"Orange juice please," he muttered, looking at the floor. The woman behind the counter passed him his drink.

"You look a bit peaky, love," she said.

Ramzi pulled his dark curls in front of his face, mumbled something and turned round.

After the bright sunlight outside, the café seemed poky and dark – but Ramzi could just about make out some figures. There were two women sitting on an old leather sofa, sipping lattes by the window. A bald man with a walking stick was doing a crossword by the door and a young man in a denim jacket was reading a newspaper in the corner. But there was no sign of Rasheed Khan!

Perhaps Shaima had been mistaken. Maybe he wasn't in here after all. Ramzi sat on a rickety chair near the window and sighed with relief. His hands were still shaking. He took a swig of orange juice and looked out of the window. Shaima's telescope was sticking out of the bush!

"HE'S NOT HERE," mouthed Ramzi, scratching his head. Shaima didn't come out so he winked a few times. No luck. Perhaps if he stuck out his tongue she'd notice.

The woman with long frizzy hair nudged her friend and they started to giggle.

Ramzi blushed. What must they think? He started to gulp down his juice when he heard the WHIZZZZ of a hand-dryer behind him. A door swung open and shut. Then a young man brushed past him. A man in a cream cotton suit. A man with jet black hair. A man wearing white suede shoes. It was Rasheed Khan! Ramzi spluttered on his orange juice.

"Are you all right, dear?" asked the woman with the big hair.

"We noticed you were a bit..." her friend sniggered, "out of sorts."

Ramzi nodded and slunk down in his chair. Being a Black Cat Detective wasn't easy. But he wasn't going to give up. No way. Out of the corner of his eye, he watched as Rasheed swung into the corner next to the man in the denim jacket. They hunched together over a newspaper and started laughing.

But Ramzi couldn't hear what they were saying. The enormous silver coffee machine was making too much noise. He needed to get closer. But how? What would a Black Cat Detective do? Suddenly, it came to him. There was a shelf of magazines just behind them. Perfect. Ramzi went over and picked up a tattered copy of *Fly Fishing Weekly*. It was the perfect size – just big enough to cover the edges of The Black Cat Detective Casebook. He pulled it from under his T-shirt and started to write down what he heard:

Man: Are you sure they're related, Rash?

Rasheed: How many Asian 'Stalks' do you think live round here, man?

Man: Good point. So, she's going to be, like, totally loaded?

Rasheed: Yeh. And much more wealthy than a bloomin' GP

Man: So you don't mind getting hitched to a bug lady?

Rasheed: She won't be a bug lady once we're married. No need. Not when we're rolling in it. Anyway, I'm gonna get rid.

Man: Of what?

Rasheed: Those bugs. Freak me out, man.

Man: Nice one. But it's not gonna be easy – with a 'Mrs' at your side.

Rasheed: That's why you're gonna do it. You owe me, remember?

The man nodded and drummed his fingers on the table. Then Rasheed lowered his voice until it was barely a whisper.

Ramzi slipped the casebook under his T-shirt, dropped the magazine on the floor behind their table and bent down to listen. He only heard a few words, but it was enough:

"... keys... laboratory... honeymoon... fire!"

Putting the magazine back on the shelf, Ramzi headed for the door. He was none the wiser about Fly Fishing but he knew a lot more about the hearts of men.

***

"You were right about Rasheed," panted Ramzi, rushing into the bush. "He's going to burn her beetle collection!"

"He's what?" shrieked Shaima.

"Yeh. When they're on their honeymoon. He's getting his friend to do it."

"You're joking! But why?" gasped Shaima.

"He totally hates bugs. He thought she was a wealthy GP, not an insectologist."

"This is *so* my fault," sighed Shaima. "I thought she'd get more replies on *Truly Deeply Muslims* if I didn't mention the 'insectologist' bit."

"What I don't get," said Ramzi, "is *why* he still wants to marry her when he knows about the beetles? It's totally weird. He thinks she's loaded."

Shaima passed Ramzi the telescope. "Take a look," she said. Rasheed and his friend had gone but they'd left an open newspaper on the table. Ramzi peered through the lens:

"I'm not that interested in money," said niqab-wearing Ms Zakiya Stalk. "I'll give some to my brother and sister. The rest will go to charity."

"So Aunty Urooj *will* be rich," said Ramzi.

"And Rasheed Khan knows! We've got to warn her! Now!" said Shaima, squeezing the telescope into her bag. "Otherwise her beetle collection will go up in smoke!"

***

They rushed back to Cinnamon Grove as fast as they could. Shaima and Ramzi burst into Number Twelve and started searching the rooms.

"Stop banging the doors!" said Mrs Stalk.

"But *Ammi*, where's Aunty Urooj?!" panted Shaima. Ramzi stumbled into the kitchen: "*Assalemu aleikum*, Mrs Stalk."

"*Wa'aleikum assalem*, Ramzi. Where are your manners, Shaima? You didn't tell me Ramzi was coming for tea."

"I'm not, Mrs Stalk. We're just…" He didn't know what to say.

"Well, if you're looking for your aunty, I'm afraid

you're too late," said Mrs Stalk, wiping Iqbal's face with a dish cloth.

"Aunty 'Rooj all gone," grinned Iqbal.

"Where? Where's she gone?" asked Shaima.

"She flew away," said Iqbal.

Shaima looked at Ramzi. "Oh no!" she gasped. "She's gone to Dusseldorf!"

"It's OK, Agent Stalk," said Ramzi. "She'll be totally safe there. He won't do anything. Not 'til she's back."

Mrs Stalk looked confused. Then she smiled and waggled her finger. "Oh, I see. You're playing some kind of game. Very good."

"It's not a game, *Ammi*," insisted Shaima. "It's a matter of life and death."

Mrs Stalk nodded and winked. "Yes, of course it is," she said.

Dad's Balancing Trick

The following morning, Dad was standing on the banister at the bottom of the stairs.

"What are you doing, Dad?" asked Ramzi.

Dad was wobbling dangerously. "I found this book in the attic," he said, waving a sky-blue book in the air.

"Careful, Dad, you'll fall!"

"No. I won't," beamed Dad. "I'm already on Stage Three."

Ramzi tilted his head upwards to read the book's cover:

REACH FOR THE SKIES:
Overcoming Vertigo in Six Simple Stages

"Dad, get down! You'll hurt yourself."

"Can't. Talk. Now," said Dad.

Ramzi chewed on his lip. "Look, Dad. You don't *have* to go up in the hot air balloon if you don't want to."

"Will. Come. Just. Need. More. 'Exposure. Treatment'. Before. 'Changing. State. Of. Mind'. "

"All right, Dad," said Ramzi. He ran under the outstretched arm and into the kitchen.

"Have you done *fajr* yet?" asked Mum. She was bobbing up and down with Baby Zed strapped to her chest whilst toasting some crumpets.

"Yeh, 'course," said Ramzi. "Have you seen Dad?"

Mum smiled. "Is he still preparing himself for lift-off?"

Ramzi nodded. "Won't he be late for work?"

"Mohamed!" yelled Mum, looking at the clock. "Get down. It's nearly half past eight."

There was a CLATTER and a THUD. Ramzi and Mum waited. When Dad staggered into the kitchen, he looked a little green. "I just need to find a bridge in my lunch hour," he said, grabbing his thermos flask.

113

"A bridge?" asked Ramzi.

"Trust the Creator, little warrior," he said. Then he kissed them all goodbye and raced out of the door.

"Will he be all right?" said Ramzi. "What does he need a bridge for?"

"More 'exposure treatment', I suppose," said Mum. "Don't worry, poppet. He loves nothing better than a challenge. Now pass me the chocolate spread."

Ramzi tucked into the chocolatey crumpet and smiled. Everything felt better when chocolate spread was melting on your tongue.

But something was niggling away inside him. Then he remembered. Rasheed Khan and the newspaper! He wanted to tell Mum. She'd know what to do.

"Mum," began Ramzi. "You know that Rasheed Khan..."

"Yes?" smiled Mum. "Mrs Stalk did mention him. Quite a looker, isn't he? What about him?"

"Well," began Ramzi. "He's got this...."

"Waaaaaaaaaa!" It was Baby Zed.

"Oh dear, she's woken up again. Sorry, love. Another time, eh?" smiled Mum.

Ramzi nodded.

Money Troubles

"They're out," shouted a voice. Ramzi was knocking on Shaima's door when he turned round to find Benjamin Butley running towards him.

"I didn't know you were back," said Ramzi. "Aren't you s'posed to be on your dad's barge?"

"S'got a leak," said Benjamin. "Had to come back to Mum's. Wanna play football? We could do sliding tackles."

"Dunno." Ramzi kicked a stone across the path. "I've gotta help Shaima with something," he said.

Benjamin Butley screwed up his nose. "Help *Shaima Stalk*? Like the 'walking encyclopaedia' needs help! Anyway, told you. They're out. Saw their car. Come on. Let's go to the park." He threw the ball at Ramzi and shouted: "HEADERS."

Ramzi leapt in the air and felt the welcome sting of leather on his forehead.

"AND HE SCORES!" yelled Benjamin Butley.

Ramzi laughed and kicked the football down Cinnamon Grove.

***

Shaima was sitting in the back of the people-carrier, 'exercising her little grey cells'. There was only one explanation for the Stalks' sudden visit to Aunty Zakiya's. The newspaper article about the Quainlong vase – it must have been true!

"She says it's a matter of great urgency," said Mrs Stalk, arranging her scarf in the overhead mirror.

"Well, it better be," said Mr Stalk. "I've taken the day off work."

"She's not one to make a fuss about nothing," said Nanna Stalk. "It's a shame Urooj isn't here. I wonder what it's all about?"

Shaima rubbed her spectacles until they shone.

When they arrived at the cottage, the door was already ajar.

"Zakiya," called Nanna Stalk. "Are you in?"

"Yes," came a distant reply. They took off their shoes and pushed past the boxes. Shaima noticed the long black *niqab* hanging by the door.

"*Alhamdulillah*, you're here," said Aunty Zakiya. She looked different this time. She was wearing pink tracksuit bottoms and a stripy top – her pony tail bobbing on one side.

"Are you all right?" asked Mr Stalk. "We got your message. What's happened?"

Aunty Zakiya kissed them all and sighed. "I suppose I should be happy," she said. "But I feel terrible."

"Why? What's happened?" asked Mrs Stalk. "What's wrong?"

Aunty Zakiya passed a rolled-up newspaper to Mr Stalk and he straightened it out. Shaima recognised the picture straight away. It was the same as the one she'd seen through the telescope. The one Rasheed had been reading at the *Café Rouge*.

117

"*Subhan'Allah!*" exclaimed Mr Stalk. "Is that a picture of you? So... you've... well, *subhan'Allah!!*"

"Pass me that," ordered Nanna Stalk. She peered through her thick glasses and scanned the words."*Alhamdulillah!*" she said, squeezing her daughter's arm. "I always said you should deal in antiques. What wonderful news!"

"But is it?" asked Aunty Zakiya.

They looked at her blankly.

"Of course it is! You've just come into millions of pounds," said Nanna Stalk, stabbing the paper."Your future is secure. How can this *not* be good news?"

"But I don't want more money," sighed Aunty Zakiya. "I don't even like money. It makes things complicated. I just like *old things*."

"She had a difficult birth," sighed Nanna Stalk, throwing the newspaper down on an antique cake-trolley. "That's why she talks such nonsense."

Mr Stalk raised an eyebrow.

"Mustafa," pleaded Aunty Zakiya. "Will you help me?"

"Of course," said Mr Stalk. "Mr Ramadan knows a lot about stocks and shares."

"No, I don't mean that. I want you and Urooj

to have it. I'll give some to charity, of course, but ..." she grabbed Mr Stalk's hand, "you could buy a bigger building for *The Spice Pot* and Urooj always needs money for research. Take it off my hands, brother. It's such a burden."

Mr Stalk looked puzzled. "A burden? Are you sure about this?"

She nodded.

"All right then, Zakiya – you're one in a million." He hugged her tight, his long black beard tickling her face.

She brushed it away. "And we can put some aside for Amin and Shaima's University fees, and pay for *Ammi*'s chiropody bills and Iqbal can have..." Aunty Zakiya paused to think.

"Can I have an ice-cream, please?" asked Iqbal.

Aunty Zakiya laughed. "Yes and Iqbal can have an ice-cream. Shaima – they're in the freezer. Go help yourselves."

Shaima nodded thoughtfully as she wandered past the cake-trolley and into the kitchen. There was a scrumpling sound of paper as she left the room, but no one noticed. Stuffing something into her *salwar kameez,* she squeezed past a grandfather clock, opened the freezer and passed Iqbal a cornet. Then, taking one for herself, she went outside.

Shaima looked at the apple trees and sighed. If only Aunty Urooj *wasn't* in Dusseldorf. If only she knew about the money. Or rather, if only she knew that *Rasheed Khan* knew about the money. Shaima peeled off the wrapper and licked the top of her walnut whip.

"LOOK AT ME!" shouted Iqbal. He was hanging upside-down from an old tree, his ice-cream dripping on to the grass.

"IQBAL – BE CAREFUL!" yelled Shaima.

"Everything's upside-down," giggled Iqbal.

"You're going to fall!" yelled Shaima.

"Wheheee!" cried Iqbal – his legs swinging in the air.

Shaima ran across the grass, grabbed his little body and plonked him on the floor. "Look at you!" she scolded. "You're *covered* in ice-cream. What's *Ammi* going to say?"

Tears welled up in Iqbal's eyes and his bottom lip began to quiver. "Iqbal all sorry. It was only an accident," he said.

Shaima slumped on to the grass next to him. "No. I'm sorry, Iqbal," she said. "It's just that... well... I think it might be all *my* fault. Everything's going wrong. I mean... if Rasheed marries Aunty Urooj and burns her special beetle collection, it'll be because of me. You've not been naughty. You're just sticky. That's all."

"Shaima," said Iqbal.

"Yeh?"

"Iqbal got good idea."

"What?" asked Shaima.

Iqbal giggled. "Shall we play monsters?"

Shaima laughed. "OK."

"Shaima..."

"Yes, Iqbal?"

"Are you a monster now?"

"GRRRRRRRRRRRR," snarled Shaima. For no one – not even Shaima Stalk – could be clever, serious and detective-like *all* of the time. She wriggled her fingers in the air and growled: "I'M COMING TO GET YOU!"

Iqbal screamed as she chased him across the buttercup lawn.

Up, Up and Away

"I can't look!" said Dad. He was sitting in the bottom of the basket with his eyes squeezed shut.

"Come on, Dad," yelled Ramzi, the wind blowing in his face. "It's awesome!"

Ramzi had always dreamed of exploring the world – but he'd never imagined that a balloon ride could be so magical. Every time it began to sink in the sky, a huge roar of fire lifted it back up again. On tiptoe, he peered over the edge of the basket. Far below, rivers twisted like silver string, houses stuck together like Lego. The world had turned into a toy town and Ramzi felt like a giant. "Dad, come and look! It's great!"

Slowly, Dad stood up. "Vertigo," he explained to Amin, "makes me... feel like I'm going to... fall through... the bottom of this thing."

"You'll be OK, Mr Ramadan," smiled Amin.

Dad nodded. "You're right. This world is just a test."

Shakily, he edged towards Ramzi, clutching the rim of the basket. Ramzi held his hand as Dad glanced at the earth below. Suddenly, everything started to swim. His knees buckled. Ramzi grabbed his waist and helped him to the side.

"Look!" said Shaima. "There's Cinnamon Grove." She was pointing at a cluster of grey houses nestled by some dark green trees.

Dad sat down again. He was looking pale.

"What are we going do?" asked Ramzi.

"We've got to distract him," said Shaima.

"How?"

Shaima's eyes began to twinkle. "Mr Ramadan," she began. "Did you know that the first things to go up in a hot air balloon were a sheep, a duck and a rooster?"

The balloon lurched and Dad closed his eyes.

"It's not working," said Ramzi.

"Patience, Agent Ramadan," whispered Shaima. She bent down in front of Dad and tried again. "Mr Ramadan – the demonstration took place outside the Palace of Versailles, right in front of Marie Antoinette."

Dad tried to smile. "A sheep, eh?"

"Yes, Mr Ramadan... and the first man to attempt flight was a *Muslim Berber* called Abbas Ibn Firnas." Dad looked up. "He was a totally famous physician *and* poet *and* musician *and* engineer *and* aviator from the Emirate of Cordoba – born in 810 AD!"

Ramzi grinned. "He was like *you*, Dad. A flying Berber!"

Very slowly, Dad grabbed the side of the balloon and stood up.

"A flying Berber, eh?" he said, puffing out his chest.

"I think you'll find it was an *Englishman*," said the man from the *Pendragon Balloon Company*.

"What?" asked Dad, turning round. It was the first time the balloon man had spoken and they all looked at him with surprise.

"I said, the first man to attempt flight was an Englishman."

Dad's face fell.

Ramzi looked at Shaima. *Please don't be wrong,* he thought.

Shaima adjusted her spectacles: "Oh, you mean Eilmer – the flying monk," she said, smiling. "Yeh – he was an Englishman. But that was in the tenth century. Way after Abbas Ibn Firnas. Eilmer made the same mistake, though." She flapped her hands behind her bottom. "No tail."

The balloon man turned the heat up and there was a sudden ROAR of flame.

"I think you've upset him," giggled Ramzi. "How do you know all this stuff, anyway?"

"Books, I guess," shrugged Shaima. "And the internet and Radio 4 and... hey, look at your dad!"

Ramzi glanced behind him. Dad had his arm round the balloon man's shoulder and was shouting over the noise of the gas.

"No offence, my friend, but you've got to admit – European history's a complete whitewash!"

Amin and the balloon man looked startled but Dad carried on. "I just don't understand it. Why do Europeans blank out other people's histories and say everything began with the Greeks? I mean, what about the Assyrians, and the Persians, and the Egyptians – not to mention the Chinese and the Indians and..."

"Agent Stalk," said Ramzi. "You are so totally cool. Dad's like *completely* forgotten about his vertigo."

Shaima shrugged and smiled.

"What happened to them, anyway?" asked Ramzi.

"Who?"

"The men without tails."

Shaima leant over and whispered in Ramzi's ear: "Well, Abbas Ibn Firnas broke his ribs and Eilmer broke both his legs. But let's not tell your dad that bit."

They both looked over at Dad. He was flapping his imaginary wings. Ramzi smiled – Shaima was *always* right.

The Wedding Sari

When Shaima Stalk ran into a red-and-gold sari at the bottom of the stairs, she knew she had to act fast.

"Careful!" yelled Aunty Urooj. Shaima unravelled herself from the sari's slippery folds and burst into the lounge.

"You're back!" Shaima exclaimed.

Aunty Urooj was sitting on Iqbal's little stool, her sleeves and trousers rolled up as if she was going for a paddle in the sea. "I was only gone for a couple of nights," she said.

"Yes, but there's a red-and-gold sari at the bottom of the stairs?!"

"I'm glad you like the colour," beamed Aunty Urooj.

Shaima blinked. "But that means..."

Mrs Stalk came into the room, carrying what appeared to be a tube for decorating cakes. "We were going to tell you the wedding's tomorrow, Shaima," said Mrs Stalk, "but you've been acting so strange lately."

"But... but..." stammered Shaima, "but... why tomorrow? What's the rush?"

Aunty Urooj blushed.

"Don't be cheeky," said Mrs Stalk.

"No. It's OK. I should have told Shaima before," said Aunty Urooj, taking Shaima's hand. "He will be your Uncle Rasheed, after all."

Shaima felt sick. "But..."

"But what?" asked Mrs Stalk, kneeling down by Aunty Urooj's bare feet.

"But... I need to go and see Ramzi." Shaima ran out of the house.

"Shaima!" said Aunty Urooj, standing up.

"Don't move!" said Mrs Stalk. "You'll spoil it."

Mrs Stalk had just started to squeeze dark brown henna onto Aunty Urooj's toes. "One smudge – and I'll have to start again."

Aunty Urooj sat down again. "Is Shaima all right?" she asked.

"Not really," sighed Mrs Stalk. "The pressure's getting too her."

"But she could do that exam in her sleep," said Aunty Urooj.

Mrs Stalk smiled. "*Insha'Allah.* Now, are you sure you want this pattern? Nanna thinks something more *conservative* might be better?"

Aunty Urooj gazed at the tiny stag beetles twisting around her ankle. "No. This will be perfect," she smiled.

***

"Ramzi! Ramzi! Aunty Urooj is back. We've got to do something! Now!" cried Shaima.

"What?" Ramzi was taking penalty kicks against garden wall.

"She's having her henna done!"

"So?" said Ramzi. "Mum's always doing that." He kicked the ball hard. "GOAL," he yelled, throwing his arms into the air and waving at the invisible crowds. "Did you see that?" he grinned.

"Boys are soooo weird," muttered Shaima under her breath. She pushed open the garden fence and grabbed the football. "Agent Ramadan, are you a member of *The Black Cat Detective Agency* or *not*? Because if you're not..."

"OK, OK," said Ramzi. "But what's the problem? She's only having some henna done."

Shaima sighed. "Ramzi Ramadan – henna fades *very quickly*. And henna has to look good for the wedding. Which means..." She looked at Ramzi expectantly, waiting for the penny to drop.

"Oh!" he said, "You mean..."

"Yes! The wedding's TOMORROW."

Without warning, Shaima grabbed Ramzi's arm and pulled him to the ground.

"Now what are you doing?" asked Ramzi.

"Shhhh!" said Shaima, putting her hand over Ramzi's mouth.

Footsteps echoed along the pavement on the other side of the wall. Ramzi mouthed the words, "Rasheed Khan?" Shaima nodded. They held their breath and waited. And waited. And waited. When they were sure he'd gone, they both stood up.

"But what's he doing here?" asked Ramzi. "I thought you said they're getting married *tomorrow*?"

"I don't know, Agent Ramdan," said Shaima. "But we've got to stop him."

Shaima started to run in the direction of her home. Ramzi did a quick tumble-roll and followed.

***

By the time they got to the doorstep of Number Twelve, Ramzi was wheezing. He hated the fist that gripped his chest. Pulling the little blue inhaler out of his pocket, he pressed the puff of air and sucked hard.

"Are you OK?" asked Shaima.

Ramzi held his breath and nodded. Then he breathed out slowly and waited for the ache inside his ribs to go. "Of course I'm OK. What's the plan?"

"Well," said Shaima, "I thought I'd just tell them the truth."

"But they won't believe you. They think you've got 'exam stress'."

"That's why *you're* going to do it, Agent Ramadan," said Shaima.

"What? Oh no, not *again*."

"Are you a Black Cat Detective or *not*?"

Ramzi sighed. "OK then. But let's wait until Rasheed comes out."

Shaima shook her head and pushed Ramzi into the house. "No. We have to do it now," she said.

***

"*Assalemu aleikum,* Mrs Stalk, Nanna Stalk, Aunty Urooj," shouted Ramzi nervously. The red-and-gold sari had gone.

"Quick, you two, come in. Shut the door," whispered Aunty Urooj. "He doesn't know I'm here. He's in the kitchen discussing honeymoon arrangements!" Her face was flushed with excitement.

They stumbled into the lounge and stared at the wet brown squiggles on Aunty Urooj's hands and feet. It reminded Ramzi of his Nanna in Algeria. She mixed lumps of brown henna on little saucers and covered her feet until they glowed.

"He mustn't see me!" giggled Aunty Urooj. "I've hidden the sari over there." She pointed at the bright red silk. "Hey, what's the matter with you two?"

Ramzi and Shaima had their backs against the door and were blinking like rabbits in the headlights.

"What?" she asked. "Don't you like it? Oh dear. Perhaps *Ammi* was right. Maybe stag beetles are too... ?"

"It's not that," interrupted Shaima. "The beetles are great. It's just..." She looked at Ramzi.

Ramzi chewed his lip. It was now or never.

"Well, we've kind of been collecting evidence..." he began. "Agent Stalk, where's the secret casebook?"

"In HQ," said Shaima. "I'll get it. Back in a minute."

Checking no one was following her, Shaima ran off to the shed.

Meanwhile, Ramzi did his best to explain. "We think," he began, "that Rasheed Khan might try and... do something bad to your beetle collection."

"What?" said Aunty Urooj in disbelief. "There is *no way* that Rasheed, or anybody else for that matter, would *ever* want to damage my beetle collection. It's one of the best in the world. What a terrible thing to say! It's unthinkable. Besides, Rasheed loves them just as much as I do!"

Shaima burst in through the French windows, the secret red casebook in her hands. "It's all true!" she said.

"I heard him," continued Ramzi. "At the *Café Rouge*. He said your beetles 'give him the creeps'. He's planning to steal your keys and his friend's going to break into your laboratory when you're on your honeymoon."

Aunty Urooj shook her head.

"Look – it's all in here," said Shaima. She unlocked The Black Cat Detectives' Secret Casebook and passed it to Aunty Urooj. "His friend is going to burn them!"

Aunty Urooj's eyes nearly shot out of their sockets! Reluctantly, she began to flick through the pages. "No, no, no," she said, shaking her head. "You've made a mistake. You're wrong. Rasheed thinks my beetles are amazing."

"But he was *pretending*. Just like he pretended to be an orphan," said Shaima.

Ramzi nodded.

"Look," said Aunty Urooj, handing the casebook

back. "If – and it's a big if – he hates beetles so much, then why on earth would he want to marry an insectologist? It doesn't make sense."

Shaima and Ramzi looked at the carpet. "It's at the back," said Ramzi.

"What is?"

"The picture of Aunty Zakiya," said Shaima, returning the bright red book.

"What's my sister got to do with it?" asked Aunty Urooj.

"Just look at the newspaper cutting," said Shaima, pointing to the article she'd sneaked off the cake-trolley.

"You see," began Ramzi, "he wants your money." There, he'd said it.

Aunty Urooj blinked. "Money?" She couldn't take it all in.

"Your money – from the sale of the vase," said Shaima.

Aunty Urooj blinked again.

"Aunty Zakiya's just sold a Quainlong Vase. It made a total fortune and she's going to give loads to you," explained Shaima.

"Yeh – like millions," said Ramzi. "We saw him

laughing about it when we were spying on him. It's all in the book."

"When you were what?" exclaimed Aunty Urooj.

Shaima fiddled with her glasses nervously. "We were worried about you, Aunty Urooj. That's why we set up *The Black Cat Detective Agency*. We followed him. We saw him reading about Aunty Zakiya. It was in the local newspaper. He knows you're going to be rich. That's why he wants to marry you. I'm so sorry."

"But..." stammered Aunty Urooj. "He knew I was an insectologist when he met me!"

Shaima looked guilty. "It's all my fault," she said. "I didn't mention the beetles on your profile. I just said you were a doctor."

"I see," said Aunty Urooj. "And I thought... well... I thought..." She looked at her feet. "I'd better go and wash this off," she said. Then she disappeared upstairs.

Ramzi and Shaima looked at each other. Being a detective was tough.

When Aunty Urooj came downstairs, she looked like an Indian princess. Her sleeves were rolled back down, but her feet and hands were bare. The dark henna had been washed away, leaving a beautiful deep orange stain. But her face was flushed with anger.

"I need to talk to Rasheed," she said, storming towards the kitchen.

***

Mrs Stalk, Nanna Stalk, Mr Stalk and Rasheed were sitting round the table. They were looking at a glossy holiday brochure while Iqbal was playing by the fridge.

The kitchen door burst open.

"Rasheed Khan," said Aunty Urooj, "answer me this. Why *exactly* do you want to marry me?"

Nanna Stalk jumped up. "Urooj, what are you doing? You shouldn't let him see you until the wedding!"

"No. I'm sorry. This can't wait. Answer the question please."

"I was just saying," smiled Rasheed, "Mauritius would be perfect. I've found us a beautiful hotel." He pointed to a gleaming white building with a turquoise pool spilling into the sea.

"I don't care about hotels and pools. *Why* do you want to marry me?"

Rasheed twitched awkwardly. "Because of your great beauty and intellect, my diamond."

"Beauty and intellect?" said Aunty Urooj, softening. "So, it's got nothing to do with *anything else*?"

"No, no, no," smiled Rasheed. "Of course not." He turned to Mr Stalk. "I don't even know how much money those vases are worth, anyway."

Mr Stalk looked at Aunty Urooj. Her mouth was hanging open in disbelief. Suddenly, Rasheed Khan realised what he'd said!

"Of c... c... course..." he stuttered, "money is of no consequence. Who needs money when they have, erm, love..."

Aunty Urooj narrowed her eyes.

"But just think," he continued, digging himself in deeper, "we'd be able to buy a big house with security gates... and have a private cinema... and my mother could come and live with us."

"Your mother? But I thought you said you were an orphan!"

Rasheed began to panic – he could almost see

the crisp, new bank notes slipping from his hands. "But, Urooj, my treasure... my mother has quite a bad cold, so I might be an orphan soon, and besides..."

"Besides? Let me tell you something, Rasheed Khan," said Aunty Urooj, fixing him with her steely glare. "*If* my sister gives me any money, I intend to donate half of it to the Beetle Benevolent Fund. The rest I will use to help my research. It will not go to you, Rasheed Khan."

"But my dearest diamond, my jewel," said Rasheed. "Why would you want to dirty your pretty little hands with those disgusting bugs? When we're married and rolling in money, there'll be no need for you to work."

Aunty Urooj gasped in horror. "So it's all true! You hate insects. And my laboratory? You *were* planning to burn it down!" Her voice became a breathless whisper.

Mr Stalk got up and stood by her side. "Now, now Urooj. We need some time to think about all this."

"No, Mustafa. Ramzi and Shaima were right about everything – they showed me their secret casebook. Rasheed Khan is a sham."

Everyone looked at Rasheed, waiting for an answer. But he couldn't speak.

"I think you'd better leave, " said Mr Stalk.

"I'm sure I could learn to *love* beetles, if you really want me to," he pleaded.

Aunty Urooj followed him to the door. "You are nothing but a lowly fraud," she said. "I should have listened to Ramzi and Shaima all along. The only thing you will ever love is yourself. Now, get out of this house!" She pointed to the door with her henna-tattooed hand.

"B...b...but," stammered Rasheed.

"Out. Now," said Mr Stalk, grabbing Rasheed's arm.

Though both very small, Nanna Stalk and Shaima – who felt jointly responsible for this whole

catastrophe – helped Mr Stalk push Rasheed through the hall. He stumbled into Cinnamon Grove and out of their lives forever.

At least, that's what Shaima wrote in The Black Cat Detectives' secret casebook.

***

"You were awesome, Aunty Urooj," said Shaima, glowing with pride.

"Yeh," nodded Ramzi. "You totally showed him."

143

Aunty Urooj forced a smile.

"I think," said Nanna Stalk, staring at the laptop suspiciously, "that he might have been some sort of *computer virus.*"

Shaima tried to explain that computer viruses don't walk about in white suede shoes, but Nanna Stalk's mind was fixed. "I've been around a lot longer than you," she said. "Now – I think we all need some tea – with extra sugar." This was Nanna Stalk's remedy for every trouble in life. She patted Aunty Urooj on the shoulder and went to put the kettle on.

Aunty Urooj looked at the clock. "I need to go," she said. Then she noticed the red-and-gold sari hanging behind the curtain and sighed.

"Why do you have to go?" asked Shaima.

"A beetle's about to emerge. And he's late," said Aunty Urooj.

Nanna Stalk looked worried. "You shouldn't be on your own. Not now. You've had a terrible shock. Why don't you take Shaima and Ramzi with you?"

"To the laboratory?" asked Shaima. She tried her best *not* to sound excited.

Aunty Urooj shrugged. "S'pose," she said, grabbing her carpet bag. But her voice was empty and hollow.

"The beetles – they're not, like, loose are they?" asked Ramzi, as they headed for the door.

"They might be," grinned Shaima mischievously.

A Beetle is Born

The smell of dank earth and musty leaves filled their nostrils as the door pushed open.

"Wow!" exclaimed Shaima. She'd never been into Aunty Urooj's laboratory before and stood on tiptoe trying to peer into one of the glass containers.

"Which one is it?" asked Ramzi, moving away from a clump of dark green branches.

"Not that one!" said Aunty Urooj. "He's over here." She was pointing at an enormous glass container with a bright light hanging overhead. Shaima ran over to look. Ramzi walked as if gravity were working against him.

"*Subhan'Allah!*" cried Aunty Urooj. "We're only just in time!"

There, on the warm brown soil, was a large white maggoty thing! Very slowly, it started to wriggle. Then, the larger end started to bulge. Something dark was pushing through its slimy surface! Ramzi felt the muscles in his legs tighten. Would they notice if he slipped out of the door? He started to edge away from the glass.

"Hold this!" said Aunty Urooj, throwing her clipboard at Ramzi's chest. Ramzi clutched it tight, like a shield.

"This is awesome!" said Shaima. She was drawing sketches of the maggoty thing's changing shape when suddenly, it stopped.

"Is it dead?" asked Ramzi.

"Of course it's not dead!" said Aunty Urooj.

They waited in silence. The huge white lump quivered. Then it wriggled down into the mud and disappeared.

"Oh no! Where's it going?" exclaimed Shaima.

"Don't worry. This is all to be expected. It's typical behaviour of a Rhinoceros Beetle," said Aunty Urooj. "It'll come back up. You can trust me on that."

They waited with bated breath. The minutes passed.

"Are you sure it's not dead?" asked Ramzi.

Aunty Urooj glared at him.

"Look!" said Shaima.

The tip of the fat white worm reappeared – shining under the light.

SHLURK. They all gasped as a sharp black horn pierced the surface like a knife. Legs and antennae unravelled and there he was – the long-awaited Rhinoceros Beetle!

"It's awesome!" squealed Shaima again.

Ramzi was speechless. And slightly sick.

Aunty Urooj smiled happily. "As he's from South America, I shall call him Salvador. He'll get much bigger, you know. Some grow as big as my hand."

Salvador was the most enormous beetle Ramzi had ever seen! Much bigger than Gulliver. In fact, he didn't really look like a beetle. He looked more like a mini-beast ready for war.

"What does he eat?" asked Ramzi nervously.

Aunty Urooj laughed. "Just rotting fruit and stuff. He won't hurt you."

"Can I hold him?" asked Shaima.

"Sure," said Aunty Urooj, lifting the lid. She picked up the enormous beetle and placed it carefully on the back of Shaima's arm. Shaima grinned. Salvador's black silhouette trembled against her turquoise *salwar kameez.*

"Wow!" giggled Shaima. "He's incredible!"

Aunty Urooj smiled with pride. "Ramzi – do you want to hold him?"

She turned round. But Ramzi was nowhere to be seen.

Aunty Urooj's Secret

The arrival of Salvador cheered Aunty Urooj up. But not for long. The fading henna was a constant reminder of dastardly Rasheed Khan.

"I'll never trust a man again," she sighed, staring at her beetle-print hands.

Everyone tried their best to make her feel better. Nanna Stalk knitted her a laboratory coat, Ramzi told her some of his best jokes and Shaima let her win at chess. But nothing worked. Aunty Urooj remained glum.

"Look what I've made you," said Mrs Stalk, carrying a steaming dish into the lounge. "It's your favourite – lamb and spinach curry."

"Not hungry," said Aunty Urooj.

"Have you heard the one about the doctor and the curtains?" asked Ramzi.

"Yes," said Aunty Urooj.

Ramzi looked at Shaima. She wasn't even *trying* to help. Her head was buried in a prospectus from *Greystone's Academy*! Ramzi went over and tapped her on the shoulder.

"Agent Stalk," he whispered. "Aren't you going to do something?"

Shaima grinned and threw the prospectus on the table. "Aunty Urooj," she said, "Why don't *you* come with us to collect Amin? He's coming home tomorrow."

Aunty Urooj shook her head. "No point," she sighed.

"Well, you can't just waste your life sitting in your laboratory, staring at a insects," said Nanna Stalk.

"What Nanna means," Shaima interupted, "is that *Greystone's Academy* is such an *old* building that it might be the perfect hiding place for Long-Horned Capricorn Beetles." She took Aunty Urooj's hand. "After all, you must be missing him."

Aunty Urooj looked up – small tears gathered in

her eyes. At last, someone had named the sadness. It was true. Gulliver was no more. He'd died only last week but Aunty Urooj had kept it to herself. Trust Shaima to work it out. Suddenly, everything made sense. So that was the ache in her heart – the loss of Gulliver – *not* the loss of Rasheed Khan.

Aunty Urooj smiled. She remembered Rasheed's silly cotton suit, his ridiculous smile and those awful white suede shoes! What had she been thinking? What a lucky escape! Thank heavens the wedding was off.

"You're right!" she exclaimed. "Rasheed was an absolute numpty. I see it now. And Gulliver can't have been the only one left. There *must* be more."

Ramzi smiled at Shaima. True. She was tiny *and* she was a girl. But she was definitely the best partner any Black Cat Detective could have. Of course, Long-Horned Capricorn Beetles have a short life expectancy – how could he have forgotten? No wonder Aunty Urooj was sad.

"Is it OK if I come too?" asked Ramzi. A trip to *Greystone's Academy* would be fun. After all, he'd won a balloon ride last time.

"Of course," smiled Mrs Stalk. She ladled the dark green curry on to plastic plates.

"That looks great," said Aunty Urooj. "I'm starving."

Dusty Corners

They didn't find a Long-Horned Capricorn Beetle at *Greystone's Academy*. Not that summer, anyway. But they did find something else. Or rather, *someone* else. It all happened underneath the staircase that spiralled into the Great Hall.

Ramzi and Shaima were peering through their Black Cat Detective magnifying glasses, helping Aunty Urooj search amongst the cobwebs. She was very excited. After all, it was the perfect habitat for Gulliver's kind. Dusty and old. But Ramzi wasn't looking very hard. His brief encounter with Salvador had made him wary. Perhaps that's why he was the first to turn round when Professor Entwistle coughed.

"AHEM."

Ramzi grinned awkwardly. What if looking for beetles under stairs wasn't allowed? But the Professor didn't look cross.

"Ah – I remember you," he said. "You're the boy who won the balloon ride. I hope it was to your satisfaction. Ramzi Ramadan, wasn't it?"

Ramzi nodded and hid his magnifying glass behind his back.

"*Well, assalemu aleikum*. It's good to see you again."

Ramzi was muttering his *salaams* back when Shaima came out from under the stairs.

"Ah! And if I'm not mistaken, it's Shaima Stalk – we've heard great things about you already."

"*Salaam*," smiled Shaima.

"And are there any more of you under the stairs?" asked Professor Entwistle, peering into the darkness.

"Only me!" said Aunty Urooj. She stood up and smiled, the top of her red hijab covered in a thin layer of dust:

"I hope you don't mind but you have such a wonderful staircase. Ramzi and Shaima were helping me look for a Long-Horned Capricorn Beetle."

"A what?!" exclaimed Professor Entwistle. "A Long-Horned ...well I never. I've been searching for one of those for years. I believe someone found one in Llanelli, you know. Most annoying. To be beaten to it."

"*Subhan'Allah*," gasped Aunty Urooj. "You mean, you've been looking for one too?"

The professor's misty blue eyes twinkled with excitement as he fiddled with his bow tie. "Indeed I have. Not very successful, I'm afraid. I'd simply *love* to find one myself. But they're such elusive little creatures. There must be one in here somewhere – what with all this ancient timber." He patted the staircase and a small fog of dust floated to the floor.

Shaima grinned. "So you have an interest in beetles *too*, Professor?"

"Oh yes – an absolute passion for them. I'm sure you'll think me strange. Most people do. But beetles are such fascinating creatures. And without them, I'm sure this world of ours would grind to a halt. May I?"

The professor took Shaima's magnifying glass and cricked his neck to look under the stairs.

It was at that moment that Ramzi realised what was happening. It was all part of Shaima's plan!

"And I suppose..." Shaima said, following Professor Entwistle under the staircase, "that *Mrs Entwistle* shares your love of beetles..."

"Good heavens, no. There *isn't* a Mrs Entwistle. I mean... obviously, there could be one... but there isn't... not that... I mean... of course..." He blushed.

"Of course," smiled Shaima. "You must be far too

busy – what with all the time you spend on your *INSECTOLOGY RESEARCH*. I read all about it in the school's prospectus."

Aunty Urooj stopped still.

"Yes," said Professor Entwistle, laughing awkwardly. "Just a little hobby of mine. I'm..." He paused mid-sentence. Something had caught his eye. He was looking at Aunty Urooj's hand as it pressed against the staircase. "My goodness," he said. "Are they stag beetles? How absolutely wonderful!"

Aunty Urooj smiled.

"Come on, Agent Ramadan," winked Shaima. "I think our work here is done."

The Butterfly Effect

With the 'Curious Case of Rasheed Khan and the Beetles' solved, there was only one thing left for the Black Cat Detectives to do. Ramzi crept down the garden path and opened the shed door to their HQ. Shaima was already inside, hiding behind the bikes.

"Were you followed?" she whispered.

"No," smiled Ramzi. "Mum's feeding Baby Zed. Have you done it?"

"Not yet. I thought I'd wait for you." Shaima looked up at the shelf. It was crammed with oil cans and tins. Ramzi stood on tiptoe and rummaged behind the paints. Yes. It was still there.

He pulled out their top secret Black Cat Detective Casebook, blew off the dust and turned the key in the lock.

"Can I do it?" asked Shaima.

"Sure," grinned Ramzi. He passed the book to Shaima and she flicked through the pages. Then she took out her pen and wrote:

Case CLOSED!

"So that's it, then," said Ramzi. "We've solved our first case."

"Yeh," sighed Shaima.

Ramzi looked thoughtful. "Funny, isn't it?" he said. "How it all kind of started when Iqbal got a chess piece stuck up his nose."

"It's called the 'butterfly effect'," said Shaima.

"What is?" asked Ramzi.

"You know... when a tiny event leads to lots of other bigger events."

"What *are* you on about?"

"*You know*," Shaima tried again. "That thing in chaos theory. You must've heard of it: when a butterfly flaps its wings in China, it can start a hurricane on the other side of the world."

Ramzi laughed. "Shaima Stalk – you are *so* totally weird."

"I am *so* not! *Everyone* knows about the 'butterfly effect'. It just means that something small can make lots of really exciting things happen."

"Yeh, right," said Ramzi, leaping around the shed pretending to be a butterfly.

Shaima scowled. "Stop making fun of me, Ramadan. You're just like the others at school."

Ramzi stopped. "I'm not... I didn't mean to... it's just that, well, I didn't understand. Tell me again. I'm really interested. Honest."

"OK," said Shaima, thawing slightly. "I'll do you a diagram." She flipped to the back of the casebook:

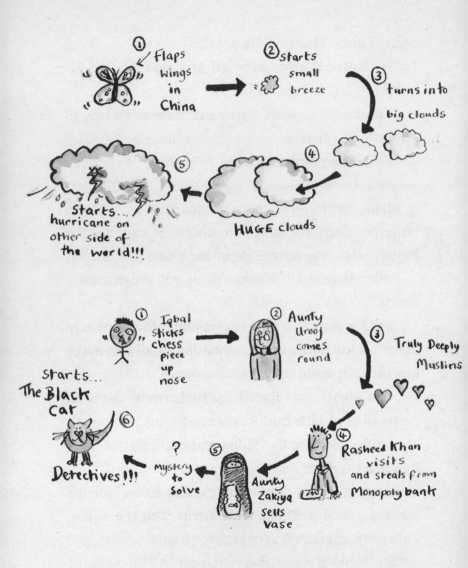

"I get it!" grinned Ramzi. "So we're Black Cat Detectives *because* Iqbal stuck a chess piece up his nose!"

"Exactly," smiled Shaima. "Something small happens in one place and makes something REALLY EXCITING happen in another. The Butterfly Effect. Simple."

"Cool," said Ramzi, nodding his head. He put the book back in its secret hiding-place behind the old tins of paint. Then, they went back into the garden.

"But what are we going to do now?" asked Ramzi, kicking a ball against the fence.

Shaima shrugged. Nothing much was happening in Cinnamon Grove. Blackbirds were cluttering up the telephone wires. Clouds were drifting over chimney pots and lazy-day Dads were mowing weed-speckled lawns. No beetles. No black cats. No butterfly effect. Just long empty days stretching across the summer like a yawn.

Ramzi slumped down on the doorstep and started picking grass. Shaima sat down next to him and, chins in hands, they stared down Cinnamon Grove.

That's when Ramzi heard it.

Hmmphhh.

"What was that?" asked Ramzi.

"What?"

"That noise!" Ramzi jumped up.

HMMMPHHH.

There it was again! "It's coming from inside that bush," said Ramzi, racing across the garden. He peered through the leaves.

A little boy was crouched between the branches, clutching his nose very tight.

"It just f...f... fell up!" said Iqbal.

"What fell up?" asked Ramzi.

"I don't even know."

"What is it?" called Shaima from the step.

Very slowly, a grin spread across Ramzi's face. "It's a butterfly, Agent Stalk. And I think it just flapped its wings!"

THE END

Salaams from the Amazon jungle!
It's amazing here. Only week
2 of our honeymoon & we've
found 36 new species!!! Robert
was stung by some bullet ants
but we're having a brilliant time.
Thanks for EVERYTHING.
See you soon
Love Aunty Urooj (Dr Stalk-Entwistle)
                              xxx
PS) I've got you both a present, btw.
Robert thinks you should call him
Maradonna!!!

to The Black Cat Detectives
c/o No.12 Cinnamon Grove
Nr Rocksford
ENGLAND
U.K.

normal
ants

a bullet ant! →
(ouch!)

A Full & Complete Explanation of... What things Mean
by Shaima Stalk

Ammi

This is what I always call my mother – even when I'm speaking in English.

Alhamdulillah

This is Arabic for *Thanks be to God* and I say it whenever I get 100% in a 'mathematically puzzling non-verbal reasoning' paper.

Assalemu aleikum

This means *Peace be Upon You* in Arabic. Muslims always say it to each other when they meet. Actually, that's not exactly correct because if someone says it to you first, then you have to say: **Wa'aleikum assalem** back. Which sounds rather difficult at first, but it really isn't when you get the hang of it.

Asr

Nanna Stalk just means 'mid-afternoon prayer'.

Astaghfirullah

Nanna Stalk is always saying **astaghfirullah.**
It means *God forgive me* and she says it quietly
when she thinks she's done something wrong.

Boureks

Mr Ramadan loves making boureks – they're very
thin, rolled-up Algerian pancakes full of mashed
potato, cumin, parsley, egg and cheese. (And when
he makes them, he normally sets the fire alarm off.
But they taste lush.)

Brother

Mr Ramadan and my dad always call each other
'brother', even when, technically speaking, they are
not. I suppose it's a little bit like 'mate'.

Dua

It's hard to explain this one. When you make 'dua',
it's a little bit like doing a prayer – but not the same
as the normal Muslim prayers – this is a little private
one where you ask God for a favour.

Eid

Eid just means *festival*. We have two of them in Islam – one after the pilgrimage to Mecca (called Eid-el-Adha) and one after Ramadan (Eid-el-Fitr). I could spend ages telling you all about these two festivals but I have to stop myself or this bit will be longer than the actual book! (Oh, and Ramadan is our fasting month.)

Fajr prayer

This is the really early prayer – the one *before* the sun comes up. Muslims do five prayers a day and they all have different names. But this one's my favourite as it makes me feel really grown-up. (All my friends are still asleep – even Ramzi Ramadan.)

Halal

Halal just means *lawful* (or *allowed for Muslims*). For example, I have to check if marshmallows are 'halal' before I let Iqbal eat them because some of them contain pork gelatine (and that is **haram** – not allowed). But it's not just about food. I'm not allowed to say rude things or be mean about people because that's 'not halal' either. Do you see what I mean?

Insha'Allah

This means *God willing* and you're supposed to say
it at the end of important things – like, 'I'm going to
study medicine when I'm a grown up, insha'Allah'.
But Nanna says it ALL the time. So, if you ask her if
she wants a cup of tea, she says 'PG tips, three sugars,
insha'Allah'.

Iqama

This is the call to prayer. Ramzi does it really well.
But Iqbal doesn't. Yet.

Jazak Allah kheir

Jazak Allah kheir means *May Allah grant you
goodness*, so it's a really nice thing to say instead of
or as well as 'thanks'.

Jilbab

Ammi always wears a really dull jilbab over her
beautiful clothes. Sometimes, I wish she'd wear
brightly coloured ones (like Marwa's mum). But she
says that's not the point. And I suppose she's right.

Masha'Allah

Masha'Allah actually means *As God wills* and
people are always saying 'Oh, Shaima is so gifted,
masha'Allah.' But it really gets on my nerves. Not
because I mind being 'gifted', but because it's totally
embarrassing.

Niqab

This is a *full veil* that covers everything apart from
your eyes – like the one Aunty Zakiya wears. I used
to think that only shy muslims wore them, but now
I don't because Aunty Zakiya has started wearing
one and she can burp the whole alphabet and do a
cartwheel (but not at the same time).

Rahemahullah

This means *May God have mercy on him or her* in
Arabic – and people normally say it about someone
when they're dead. So it's a bit sad, really. But at
least they haven't forgotten about them. (The dead
person, I mean.)

Rakats

These are the movements that we do during prayer.
And as there are five prayers a day (containing 17

compulsory rakats, 3 almost essential ones, and 20 slightly optional ones), one can safely summarise that most praying muslims do 40 rakats a day.

Salaams
Giving salaams just means giving Muslim greetings.

Salem
This means *Peace*. It's like saying 'Hi'. Sort of.

Salat
This is just the word for *prayer* and there's nothing mathematical about it.

Salwar Kameez
This is the traditional outfit worn by men and women (and boys and girls, obviously) in lots of parts of the world – it consists of baggy trousers and a longish top. Mine always have loads of sequins on because Ammi buys them when we're in Pakistan.

Subhan'Allah
I love saying 'Subhan'Allah'. It means *God is glorious* and is way better than 'Wow!'

You will need:

* A name for your Detective Agency.

* A **Headquarters**, to be
known as 'the HQ'.
(Perfect places include: a shed,
a cupboard under the stairs or
an airing cupboard.)

* A tall glass.
(For listening through walls
and floorboards.)

* A magnifying glass or
telescope.

* Some invisible ink pens.
(But if times are hard,
pencils and rubbers will do!)

* A secret casebook.

(If you need extra security, try and get one with a lock. If this isn't possible, just write 'Do not open' and 'Dangerous' on the front.)

* ID Cards.

(Of course, any good detective should also have a supply of false ID cards – make as many as you need.)

* Oh, and finally... detectives need at least one partner and one mysterious case to solve!

Good Luck!

ACKNOWLEDGEMENTS

Lots of wonderful people helped me to write this book – even if they didn't know it!

My parents – who read to me as a child and inspired my love of stories

My children – who made me laugh and shared me with my lap-top

My friends – who made me coffee and helped me meet my deadlines

My designer – who brought out the best in my illustrations

And finally, special thanks go to my patient and generous editor – Janetta Otter-Barry – who let me tell my story but made sure that I did it well.

As a child, WENDY MEDDOUR spent most of her time
in the airing cupboard reading books. Huddled up
behind the boiler, she dreamt of being a cartoonist,
a comedienne and a football player.
Unsure how to go about it, she became an English
lecturer instead – one that gave funny lectures,
doodled in the margins and knew the off-side rule.
Since leaving the safety of the airing cupboard,
she has acquired a doctorate, an Algerian husband,
four children, a wobbly old house in Wiltshire,
a farm in the Berber mountains and a huge cat
called Socrates (that many suspect is actually a goat).
Wendy's début novel, *A Hen in the Wardrobe,*
has already garnered critical success – winning the
John C. Laurence Award for writing that improves
relations between races, taking first place in the Islamic
Foundation's International Writing Competition, and
being shortlisted for the Muslim Writers' Award 2011.

**Look out for another funny adventure
in the CINNAMON GROVE series**

*...................g at night
......................in pyjamas
has ....y, climbing trees
.....................oking for
a ....o could it be?
.....................d?*

But I...................he's homesick,
and...................whole family
t...................n Algeria.
Can th...................Vise Man of the
Moun...................sert help Dad –
.....................et plan?